MONSTROUS MATCHMAKERS

WELCOME TO

PECULIAR, PENNSYLVANIA!

A PERFECTLY NICE AND
NOT-AT-ALL CREEPY PLACE TO LIVE

WITCHES OF PECULIAR

MONSTROUS MATCHMAKERS

LUNA GRAVES

ALADDIN
NEW YORK LONDON TORONTO SYDNEY NEW DELHI

ALADDIN

An imprint of Simon & Schuster Children's Publishing Division
1230 Avenue of the Americas, New York, New York 10020
First Aladdin paperback edition November 2022
Text copyright © 2022 by Simon & Schuster, Inc.
Illustrations copyright © 2022 by Laura Catrinella
Also available in an Aladdin hardcover edition.

For information about special discounts for bulk purchases,
please contact Simon & Schuster Special Sales at 1-866-506-1949
or business@simonandschuster.com.
The Simon & Schuster Speakers Bureau can bring authors to
your live event. For more information or to book an event contact
the Simon & Schuster Speakers Bureau at 1-866-248-3049 or visit our
website at www.simonspeakers.com.
Book designed by Heather Palisi
The text of this book was set in Really No. 2.
Manufactured in the United States of America 1022 OFF
2 4 6 8 10 9 7 5 3 1
Library of Congress Cataloging-in-Publication Data
Names: Graves, Luna, author.
Title: Monstrous matchmakers / by Luna Graves.
Description: First Aladdin paperback edition. | New York : Aladdin, 2022. |
Series: Witches of Peculiar | Summary: After noticing Yvette, the principal of
YIKESSS (Yvette I. Koffin's Exceptional School for Supernatural Students), has
been rather cranky recently, twin witch sisters Bella and Dee decide to cheer her
up by bringing a little romance into her life.
Identifiers: LCCN 2022005900 (print) | LCCN 2022005901 (ebook) |
ISBN 9781665914284 (pbk) | ISBN 9781665906272 (hc) |
ISBN 9781665906289 (ebook)
Subjects: CYAC: Twins—Fiction. | Sisters—Fiction. | Witches—Fiction. | Magic—
Fiction. | Middle schools—Fiction. | Schools—Fiction. | LCGFT: Paranormal
fiction. | Novels.
Classification: LCC PZ7.1.G7325 Mo 2022 (print) | LCC PZ7.1.G7325 (ebook) |
DDC [Fic]—dc23
LC record available at https://lccn.loc.gov/2022005900
LC ebook record available at https://lccn.loc.gov/2022005901

MONSTROUS MATCHMAKERS

CHAPTER 1

A black cat in a green collar moves through the shadows down Franken Lane, his fur illuminated by the dim light of the crescent moon. There are no lamps on this street, nor anywhere else inside the gates of Eerie Estates. The supernatural creatures who call this neighborhood home much prefer the darkness.

At the end of the road, the cat makes a right onto Stein Street, then ducks behind a row of shrubs and disappears. It's his piercing yellow eyes that give him away again a few minutes later, when he emerges two blocks westward, on the front lawn of the black house at 333 Quivering Court. He walks up the path to the porch and then hops onto the sill of an open window, where he can hear muffled voices and see the flickering blue glow of the living room TV. After pausing a moment to lick his paw, he slinks inside, and the window closes behind him.

On the other side of the wall, the young witch Bella Maleficent sits cross-legged on the couch in her bright green pajamas, with a bowl of popcorn in her lap. She leans forward, her eyes glued to the TV. To her left her sister, Dee Maleficent, slouches between two cushions, scrolling on her green eyephone while her feet rest on the black coffee table in front of her. The cat jumps down from the windowsill onto the back of the couch, and then crawls over Dee's shoulder to rest in her lap.

"There you are, Corny boy." Dee scratches behind Cornelius's ears and kisses him on top of the head. "I thought Eugene might've kidnapped you."

In the months since Cornelius came to live with them, he's gotten quite comfortable venturing around their gated community on his own. Eugene even texted the twins an hour ago that the cat had shown up on his doorstep to say hello.

Bella reaches down absently and grabs a handful of popcorn, then shoves the whole thing into her mouth. *"Ugh,"* she groans between chews. On the screen a woman with hair as red as the crushed velvet couch she sits on is pleading her case. "Serafina'll say anything to get a broom."

Dee puts down her eyephone and focuses on the TV. The twins are watching *Which Witch Is the One?*, their favorite supernatural matchmaking show. On this episode Alistair must take two contestants on a single date and then eliminate the one he likes the least.

"I could really see myself falling in love with him," says Serafina, one of the witches chosen for the date. She's speaking to the camera in a confessional-style setting. *"From day one I've trusted in this process, and I've been one hundred percent genuine. I think Alistair can feel that I'm here for the right reasons."*

From his place drying dishes in the kitchen, they hear their dad Ron snort. "Yeah, right. She's there to become WitchStitch famous."

"Totally, Pop," Bella agrees. She reaches for more popcorn, but her hand hits the bottom of the bowl. She uses her pointer finger to zap it full of a fresh batch, and is pleased when every kernel is perfectly popped, no burnt pieces to be seen. Since their disastrous first day at YIKESSS, with practice the twins have been able to master simple spells with a much lower rate of chaos or destruction.

"So what?" Dee says. "That doesn't mean she isn't there to find love, too."

"That's right, honey," says their dad Antony, appearing in the doorway between the kitchen and living room. "We shouldn't judge other creatures before we get to know them."

"Come on, Dad. She *wants* us to judge her," Bella argues. "Why else would she have gone on supernatural television to find love?"

The camera switches to the other contestant, Helena. *"When I started this journey, my cauldron was empty. Then Alistair filled it up. I know it's taken me a little longer than most of the other witches here to let down my walls, but now that I have . . ."* She pauses to wipe a tear from her cheek and compose herself. *"I don't want to go home tonight. Alistair has my heart."*

"Why does everyone have to be so cheesy?" Dee says, checking her phone and then immediately putting it down again. "Nobody talks like this in real life."

"Love makes people do strange things," Ron

says, joining Ant in the doorway. "Look at your dad and me. I moved to the *suburbs* for him."

Ant smiles and shakes his head. "The Enchanted Forest was no place to raise a family."

"You were right," Ron says, putting an arm around his husband. Over time, ghosts naturally become more solid around people they love. In the comfort of his own home, Ant is so solid that he can almost pass for human. "What else is new?" They exchange a quick kiss, and Bella and Dee both groan.

"Right in front of us?" Bella says. "Unbelievable."

"So embarrassing!" Dee adds.

Their dads look at each other and laugh, and the twins exchange a small smile. Bella and Dee would never admit it to Ant and Ron, but they know how lucky they are to have two parents so in love.

"Bed in ten minutes," Ant says. He moves across the living room, toward the stairwell in the foyer.

Ron shuts off the lights in the kitchen. "Good night, girls," he says, following Ant. "We love you."

"Love you," the girls both say at the same time.

Bella waits until their dads get all the way up the stairs before she smirks at Dee. She knows what her sister is looking for every time she checks her phone. Or rather, *who*.

"I'll bet you'll be just as *in lurv* as Dad and Pop after your movie date tomorrow."

Dee feels her cheeks heat up. Over the weekend, Sebastian visited the pharmacy while Dee was stocking shelves and told her about the new *Space Wars* movie that just came out. He said he was seeing it with a couple of friends on Tuesday afternoon at the Manor Theater and asked if she would like to come along. In a bout of nerves Dee stammered that *actually* she and her friends were planning to see that movie on Tuesday too. What were the odds! They agreed to meet there and then exchanged phone numbers, *just in case*. So far she hasn't received so much as a text, but that could change at any moment.

"It's not a *date*," Dee says, stroking Cornelius's back and smiling to herself. "It's a friendly gathering. That's why you're coming."

"Right," Bella says. "And I'll be there for you, of course. But, Dee, you know you don't need me. You never have trouble thinking of what to say when Sebastian comes to visit you at the pharmacy."

"I know," Dee says. "But that's when it's just the two of us. This time his human friends will be there. What if I say the wrong thing?"

"You won't," Bella assures her. "Charlie and Eugene, on the other hand—"

Hearing Eugene's name, Cornelius lifts his head and meows. He gives Dee a meaningful look.

"What is it, buddy?" Dee looks at Bella. "I think he needs to tell us something about Eugene."

"Wait, Alistair is about to give out his

broom!" Bella squeals, returning her full attention to the TV, where the three witches are seated on a picnic blanket in the woods. "Cornelius can tell us during the commercial."

"This was not an easy decision to make," says Alistair in an accent veering toward Hungarian. *"You've both sacrificed so much to come on this journey with me, and you've trusted the process even through times of uncertainty. Serafina, I love how easily we click. You make me laugh, and we have so much fun together, but there's still a part of me that worries you're not ready for commitment. And, Helena, it has been such an incredible experience getting to know you. I've seen how much you've tried to open up these last couple of weeks, and I've appreciated—"*

"Jeepers creepers," Bella groans. "Get on with it already!"

"But I do feel like there's still a part of you that you're holding back. You've lowered your walls, but you haven't knocked them down completely. I need a witch who isn't afraid to show me who they really

9

are. That being said . . ." Alistair turns to Serafina. *"Serafina, will you accept this broom?"*

Bella and Dee gasp. A kernel of popcorn falls out of Bella's mouth.

Serafina smiles wide. *"I will."* She takes the red broom. Then Alistair picks up his own broom, and the two fly away together holding hands, leaving Helena behind as she bursts into tears. The show cuts to commercial.

"No, he didn't!" Bella says, at the same time Dee says, "Big mistake, Alistair!"

"Meow!" Cornelius insists, looking from Dee to Bella.

"Okay, okay." Dee holds up a finger and zaps a notebook and pen onto the coffee table. Cornelius jumps from the couch onto the table, picks up the pen with his tail, and starts writing.

"Wow," Bella says, peering around the cat. "Your lessons with him are really starting to pay off."

"That's because he's the smartest boy in the whole world, *yes he is*," Dee coos. It's normal for witches to find creative ways to communicate with their familiars, but not many can successfully teach them to write. Such a task requires great patience and trust from both parties.

Bella, still watching Cornelius, cocks her head. "Is that supposed to say 'Eugene'?"

Dee sits up and takes the note, which looks like it was written by a small child. "He's still getting the hang of it," she reminds Bella, and then she reads the note out loud. "It says, 'You-jeen grounded. No movy.'"

Dee squints at the paper. "I think that means Eugene is grounded and can't go to the movies tomorrow."

Cornelius meows happily at his job well done.

Bella scratches him on the head and then pulls her pink eyephone out of her pajama pocket. When the eye at the top of the screen opens, she says, "Call Eugene. Speakerphone."

Eugene picks up on the third ring. "Yes, I'm grounded," he says instead of hello. "For a week. The TrashEater6000 sort of backfired.

Two weeks' worth of trash exploded all over the kitchen." He lets out a heavy sigh. "Who'd have thought a machine could get indigestion?"

"So you can't come with us to the movies?" Dee whines. "But I need moral support!"

"Sorry, Dee. Nobody's more bummed than me. I love *Space Wars*." Eugene is obsessed with anything involving flying and laser beams.

"What about the flyball game on Friday?" Bella says. "It's my first game as scream team captain, and we're debuting some routines that will *really* get the crowd roaring."

"I'll try my best to be there. Maybe Mom will lighten my sentence for good behavior," Eugene says. "Speaking of which, I've gotta get back to cleaning up. Part of my punishment is that I have to get rid of the trash myself, instead of asking one of you to spell it away for me. Mom's got one of her eyes on the table, watching me."

Bella wrinkles her nose, grateful that neither of their dads is a zombie.

"Okay," she says. "See you tomorrow at school." She hangs up.

"What a bummer." Dee slouches into the couch again as *Which Witch Is the One?* returns from commercial break. "At least you and Charlie will still be there." She scoops a handful of popcorn from the bowl on Bella's lap. "Maybe you'll even hit it off with one of Sebastian's friends."

"His human friends?" Bella scoffs. "Not likely."

"Come on, Bella," Dee urges. "Remember what Dad said? Don't judge a creature before you get to know them. Maybe they'll surprise you."

"I'm never surprised," Bella says. "Especially not by humans."

On the TV, Helena is crying in the back seat of a carriage. *"I've never let down my walls like this before, and it was all for nothing. Will I ever love again?"*

"Maybe you just need to let down your walls," Dee teases. Both sisters laugh, but deep down

Dee thinks there might be some truth to the idea. She wouldn't admit that to Bella, though. When it comes to matters of the heart, Bella can be more tightly wound than a mummy.

"Girls," they hear Ron calling out from his room upstairs. "You know what time it is."

"Boo," Bella calls out, and then points a finger at the TV and zaps it off. They don't need to bother trying to be sneaky by lowering the volume. As a werewolf, Ron has excellent hearing.

From his place on the coffee table, Cornelius meows and pushes the notebook forward with his paw. Dee picks it up and sees that he's written something else.

Giv catnip plees.

～•→ CHAPTER 2 ←•～

The next day the twins take their seats in Potions class to find their professor, a troll named Professor Daphne, writing the words *Cup of Cheer* on the board at the front of the room.

Dee sighs in relief. "We finally get to make something happy."

Bella and Dee's Potions class is in the middle

of their unit on mood-altering potions. Yesterday they learned how to brew the recipe for Sips of Sadness, which is so potent that one small whiff can cause twenty-four hours of gloom. Just ask their classmate Jeanie, who forgot to put on her mask and accidentally inhaled the vapors from her cauldron. Jeanie's mother had to pick her up at lunch after nearly two hours of uncontrollable crying.

"Yawn," Bella says, pushing her cauldron out of the way to rest her elbows on the table. She closes her eyes. "I could brew this in my sleep. Wake me up when we get to shape-shifting."

The raven perched in the corner by the door lets out a loud squawk, making the girls jump in their seats. The bird waits until it has the full attention of the class, and then opens its beak to project Principal Yvette Koffin's voice.

"Excuse the interruption, Professor Daphne," the principal says. "But I wanted to ensure that all of your students are properly masked before brewing today."

Professor Daphne frowns and crosses her arms. True to the nature of trolls, she's perpetually grumpy and has a problem with authority. She likes it even less when her own authority is questioned. "As always, they will be masked when the lesson begins."

When Principal Koffin speaks again, her tone is sharper. "Considering what happened yesterday"—several pairs of eyes in the room flick toward Jeanie, who slouches behind her cauldron in embarrassment—"that's not exactly a guarantee, is it?"

A dark cloud passes over Professor Daphne's face, and the twins exchange a nervous look. Their professor's nickname during medieval times used to be Daphne the Defiler, and she had quite the reputation before settling down to teach at YIKESSS. When she gets angry, she'll pick up whatever is closest to her and throw it a great distance. It doesn't matter what—or in the case of one student from the YIKESSS class of 1968, *who*.

"I appreciate your *concern*, Yvette," Professor Daphne spits, not sounding appreciative at all. "But I know how to lead my class."

"It doesn't seem that way to me," Principal Koffin snaps back. "In fact, it *seems* like you couldn't lead a ghoul to a graveyard, even if it gave you a map."

For a moment the room is shocked into silence. Everyone is used to Principal Koffin's strictness, but they've never heard her be so unnecessarily mean before—not to anyone, but especially not to Daphne the Defiler.

Professor Daphne lets out a roar and stomps toward the exit, leaving the floor indented in her wake. She kicks down the door, knocking it off its hinges, and continues roaring into the hallway.

Through the raven the class can hear Principal Koffin's heavy sigh. "Turn to page forty-two in your textbooks and begin brewing," she instructs. "But first, masks *on*. Is that understood, Jeanie Jenkins?"

At the table behind Bella and Dee, Jeanie looks down and nods.

"I can't hear you!"

"Yes, ma'am," Jeanie says quickly. The raven closes its mouth, ending the broadcast. It takes a few moments for the students to relax and start chattering among themselves again.

"Okay," Dee says. She pulls her textbook out of her bag. "Is it just me, or did Principal Koffin wake up on the wrong side of the tower today?"

"She definitely seems crankier than usual," Bella agrees, zapping her textbook open to the correct page. "I said hi to her this morning when I saw her in the hallway, and she totally ignored me." Then Bella perks up with an idea. "Hey, maybe if I give her my Cup of Cheer, she'll give me extra credit?"

"Listen to that, Jeanie," says Crypta Cauldronson from behind the twins. "Bella is trying to cheat to get ahead. What else is new?"

"Poor Crypta," Bella says to Dee without bothering to turn around. "Still bitter that I was voted captain of the scream team and she wasn't." She flicks her ponytail over her shoulder in satisfaction. The election was held on Friday afternoon at the flyball field, and to the surprise of Bella and Crypta, Bella won by a landslide.

Crypta snorts. "I know you cheated. What did you offer them in exchange for their votes? Magic mice? Contraband pixie dust?"

Dee, who has been sneakily checking her phone, pockets it and turns around. "Crypta, you know Bella wouldn't bribe the squad for votes. That's unethical."

"No," Crypta says. "That's politics." She narrows her eyes at Bella. "I'll figure out how you did it somehow. Just wait."

Suddenly Argus, Principal Koffin's telepathic four-eyed crow, sweeps into the room and perches on the back of Professor Daphne's desk chair. It seems the principal sent him to keep watch over the class while Professor Daphne lets out her anger. As if the bird senses the tension coming from their corner of the room, his eyes land on Bella and Crypta.

"Jealousy is an ugly emotion, Crypta," Bella whispers. "Keep it up, and you'll be greener than the Wicked Witch of the West." She turns to Dee. "Okay. Let's brew."

Bella puts on her safety mask and then conjures orange sparks to ignite a small, controlled fire underneath the cauldron. She squints down at the instructions in the textbook. "Let's see, we need to start with two teaspoons of crushed lavender, a vial of dill, and some bottled baby giggles. Dee, can you get that stuff from the supply closet while I heat the cauldron?"

Dee doesn't reply. Bella glances up to find her smiling down at her eyephone, mask still off.

"Dee, hello?" Bella waves her hand in front of her sister's eyes. "Are you even listening? Put your mask on!"

"Sorry," Dee says, though she doesn't sound it. She hurries to put her mask over her nose and mouth. "What do you need?"

Bella cocks her head. "What are you looking at?" Without waiting for a response, she snatches Dee's phone out of her hands.

"Hey!" Dee tries to take it back, but Bella, the slightly taller twin, holds it just out of reach. After a few seconds of struggling, Dee gives up and Bella smiles, satisfied. Then she looks at the screen, and her smile quickly disappears.

"You're texting Sebastian?" Bella practically shouts. She isn't sure what's more upsetting: the fact that her sister is being so careless with the rules—which clearly state no texting during class—or that Dee has been keeping this a secret from her. "Do you know what will happen if Professor Daphne sees? Your phone will get punted to the other side of Peculiar."

Bella's eyes skim the exchange. Sebastian texted first, just this morning. Can't wait for the movie later ☺. Dee replied, Same!!! ☺. They established a meeting time at the Manor Theater, and then Sebastian asked what her favorite movie snacks are. And in case ur wondering, he added, I'm a Milk Duds kinda guy.

Bella shoves the phone back into Dee's hands. "That settles that. You hate Milk Duds."

"Well," Dee says, "I don't think I've ever tried them."

Bella groans. "Dee, focus!" She snaps her fingers in front of Dee's face. "We have a potion to brew! Sebastian will still be there when we're done."

"Sebastian Smith?" Crypta chimes in, putting a hand over her chest as if in shock. "Mayor Boris Smith's son?"

Dee and Bella look at each other, their faces expressionless. If Crypta knows that Dee was texting a human, that means soon the whole school would know too.

"You shouldn't be texting the human mayor's son," Crypta chides. "You're putting us all at risk of exposure."

"It's none of your business, Crypt Keeper," Bella says.

"Actually"—Crypta raises her brow—"if it involves supernatural-human relationships, it *is* my business. Or should I say"—she leans across the table with a smug little smile—"my *mother's* business."

Bella whips her head around. "You wouldn't."

Crypta shrugs. "I might." She looks down at her textbook, feigning nonchalance. "Unless, of course, I'm too busy with all my duties as captain of the scream team."

Bella practically jumps out of her seat. "Over my undead body!"

Dee glances around the cauldron at Argus the crow. He's watching them, which means Principal Koffin probably is too.

"Fine." Crypta crosses her arms. "Co-captain?"

"Come on, Crypta," Dee sighs, keeping her voice down. "That's low, even for you."

"Maybe so," Crypta says. "But I'll go as low as I need to in order to get what I want. That's the difference between you and me."

Over at Professor Daphne's desk Argus the crow squawks in their direction. It's a warning, Dee is pretty sure. *"Okay,"* she says, picking up her textbook. "What ingredients did we need again, Bella?"

But Bella doesn't answer. She's too busy scowling at Crypta with her fists clenched. Dee can see angry red sparks shooting out from between Bella's knuckles.

Dee puts a calming hand on Bella's shoulder, though her own heart is pounding hard in her chest. "Bells, breathe," she says. "Let's get back to the potion. The cauldron fire has almost gone out."

Bella hesitates for a moment. Then, snapping out of it, she blinks and relaxes her fists. "Right," she says, returning to stoking the cauldron. "We need lavender, dill, and baby giggles, stat!"

Dee nods once, satisfied. She knows that the only thing strong enough to distract Bella from her rage is the threat of a bad grade. Dee hurries over to the supply closet and rushes to acquire the necessary ingredients. She hopes that if she throws herself into the task, perhaps she won't have time to think about what her new-found friendship with Sebastian may cost her sister—not to mention the entire supernatural community in Peculiar. And even scarier: the fact that despite everything she knows, she still doesn't want to give Sebastian up.

She returns to the table to find Bella eye level with the flames at the base of the cauldron, coaxing them into submission. Her green irises are reflecting a watercolor of oranges and reds as she concentrates. "Start with the dill," Bella instructs. "Then the baby giggles to dull the sadness, then two teaspoons of lavender for inner peace."

Dee does as she's told. When brought to a boil, the dill produces a purple steam, which the baby giggles soften to a pale pink. Even behind her mask, Dee can't help but smile when she sprinkles them in. Bella smiles too, though not because of the giggles. The potion is coming along perfectly. They're well on their way to an A+.

As Dee prepares to add the lavender, she feels her eyephone buzz in her pocket. *Not now, Sebastian,* she thinks, though she can't help but feel the bats in her stomach anxiously taking flight. In a few hours she will be with Sebastian at the movies—maybe even sitting next to him. What if he tries to hold her hand? She blushes at the thought, hoping that if Bella notices, she chalks it up to heat from the flames.

Dee dumps two tablespoons of lavender into the cauldron. Then the potion darkens, and the bubbles start to build up at an angry rate.

"Hmm." Bella frowns, confused. She lets her sparks sizzle on her fingers, lowering the flame, but it does no good. The bubbles continue to rise until they spill over the edge of the cauldron and onto the table, staining their textbooks and filling the room with a mood-numbing steam.

Bella looks at Dee. "What happened?"

"It wasn't my fault!" Dee looks at the measuring spoon in her hand. "The recipe called for—"

"Two *teaspoons*," Bella says, her eyes narrowing in on the spoon. "That's a tablespoon."

Dee deflates. "Oops." Behind them Crypta snickers.

"Jeepers creepers." Bella rubs her temples. There's no way they'll have time to clean this up *and* brew a satisfactory potion from scratch. Like her textbook, her perfect record will be stained.

Without missing a beat Argus flaps his wings and soars out of the room. A few moments later Principal Koffin comes barreling through the doorway.

"That's quite enough," she says, widening her wings behind her. She looks a bit unlike herself, Bella notices. Her red pantsuit is wrinkled, and her bun, usually so pristine that there isn't a hair out of place, appears unkempt and frizzy.

"Donna Maleficent," Principal Koffin's voice booms. "Not only have you brought failure upon yourself and your sister today"—hearing the word "failure" makes Bella drop her hands and widen her eyes in horror—"but your carelessness has created a noxious gas that could have harmed your classmates. What do you have to say for yourself?"

"I didn't do it on purpose," Dee says, taken aback by Principal Koffin's extreme reaction to such a small mistake. "I'm sorry."

"Look me in the eye when you are talking to me, girl!" Principal Koffin says.

"I'm *sorry*!" Dee says again, looking up warily. "I mean, all I did was spill a little bit of cheer. Is that really so bad? I'll clean our cauldron, and everything will go back to normal."

"You dare talk back to me?" The principal's wings extend even farther, which only happens when she is at her most vengeful. A few students at the front of the classroom cower back.

"Dee," Bella whispers. "Ix-nay on the acktalk-bay."

Dee furrows her brow. "What?"

"Very well," Principal Koffin continues. Her eyes are dark and unrelenting. "You'll clean your cauldron, and all the others on the grounds, in detention after school today."

Dee sits back in shock. YIKESSS probably has at least a hundred cauldrons. "But—but that will take hours!" And she has plans with Sebastian!

"Perhaps you should have thought of that before," the principal says.

Bella slowly raises her hand. "Um, Principal Koffin? Since I wasn't the one who messed up the proportions, do you think maybe I could have another chance to brew the potion?" She smiles guiltily at Dee and adds, "No offense. You know I'm on your side."

Principal Koffin raises her chin and looks down her nose at Bella. "There will be no second chances today." Bella slumps into her seat, and the principal looks at Dee again. "I'll see you back here at three o'clock, sharp." With one final scowl and a *whoosh* of her wings, she sweeps out the door.

CHAPTER 3

Cleaning cauldrons? Majorly nasty! I think I'd rather be grounded.

In Humans 101, while they're supposed to be reading about sewing machines, Dee reads a note from Eugene under her desk. She sighs and zaps her reply onto the paper in purple ink.

The worst part is that I have to bail on Sebastian.

Bella, Charlie, will you two still go to the movies so he doesn't think I hate him?

Dee uses her magic to fold the note into a tiny butterfly and sends it fluttering over to Bella. When Bella reads it, she lets out a small but pointed snort.

No way, Bella replies in black ink. She's still miffed at Dee for being so clumsy with the proportion of lavender, and for giving Crypta something to blackmail them with. *I'm not hanging out with humans without you!* Bella spells her note into a tiny comet and sends it shooting to the back of the room, where Charlie sits.

If Bella isn't going, I'm not going alone! Charlie adds. *What if there's a scary part, or something jumps out at me, and I accidentally shape-shift?* They use their new compulsion powers to add legs to the note and make it scurry over to Eugene.

Still bogus of Koffin to give you detention for a little cauldron spill, Eugene writes. *I mean, considering she didn't even give you detention when you nearly burned down the school in Spell Casting . . .*

He flicks the note to Dee.

I know, she replies. *Something's up with her. But what?*

The paper butterfly begins its journey to Bella, but halfway there it stops midair and disintegrates.

"Dee, Bella," Professor Belinda says, barely looking up from the scrolls on her desk. Every head in the room turns toward them. "Charlie and Eugene. You know the rules about notes. Principal Koffin's office, now."

"Wait!" Bella sits up straight. "Can't we work something out?" Professor Belinda raises one skeptical eyebrow, and Bella elaborates. "Principal Koffin is scary today. And *not* in a good way."

Professor Belinda tucks a strand of long dark hair behind her ear and ignores Bella's plea, though something in her eyes suggests she doesn't disagree with Bella.

"I'll give the principal notice that you're on your way," the professor says simply, and then returns her attention to the stack of scrolls on her desk.

The four friends make their way to Principal Koffin's tower office, Bella grumbling with her arms crossed every step of the way.

"Great, just *great*," she says. "I was supposed to be at the top of the Horror Roll this quarter, and now that's going to be ruined."

"At least you can try again next quarter," Eugene says, his ears drooping. "When Mom hears about this, her head is gonna roll. I'll probably be grounded forever."

"You don't know that," Charlie says. "Maybe Principal K will let us off with a warning?"

Even Dee looks skeptical. "I don't know. You should have seen her this morning. She was . . ." She trails off, thinking of the best way to describe the frenetic aura that surrounded their principal. "Stressed out! And *mean*."

"She definitely wasn't herself," Bella says as the group turns into the main corridor. Suddenly Dee lets out an ear-piercing scream.

Waiting around the corner is Vice Principal Augustus Archaic, and he's stretched his ghostly face into a big, sinister grin. He giggles. "I got you!" he says, putting his hands on his cheeks and pushing his face back to its normal proportions. "You were so frightened!"

"Good one, VP," Eugene says, grinning, as Charlie hides behind him, flapping their wings in bat form.

"Sorry, Vice Principal, but this really isn't a great time," Dee says. "We're on our way to Principal Koffin's office."

The vice principal's face turns grave. "Oh, dear me," he says, and then floats to the side. "Well, best be onward. And good luck to you all."

None of the friends like the sound of that.

Several minutes later the group reaches the top of the long, winding staircase that leads to Principal Koffin's tower office. Bella, ahead of the pack, walks up to the wooden door and taps the iron knocker three times. The door creaks open on its own, and one by one the friends step inside.

"Man, I'm out of shape," Eugene huffs, bringing up the rear. "I've never actually been here. I didn't know there'd be so many stairs." When he steps into the office, the door closes behind him.

"She's not here," Bella says, looking around. "Neither is Argus."

"Leaving her office unattended doesn't seem like Principal K," Charlie says, their red eyes gazing up at the tall windows, the towering bookcases. They let out a sigh of admiration. "I bet there's lots of secrets in these books. You know, I read over the summer that those stairs were built to slow down enemies if they ever try to break in."

"What kind of enemies?" Eugene says, kneeling to study a rusted contraption that looks like some sort of medieval machine.

"Humans, obviously," Charlie says. "Monsters have magic. They don't need to take the stairs."

"Great point." Eugene stands up. "Any one of you could have flown me to the top."

"If I had known you were going to complain so much, I would have," Bella says. She sits down on the bench in the center of the room. "This is the worst day *ever*."

Dee is quiet, hovering by a small portrait hanging near Principal Koffin's desk. She feels responsible that they all ended up here. Even though it was *technically* Bella who sent the first note, they had been discussing Dee's misstep in Potions. If she had only paid more attention to which measuring spoon she picked up—if *only* she weren't such a klutz—she could still be going to the movies after school.

"What am I going to say to Sebastian?" Dee looks around at her friends. "I obviously can't tell him the truth."

"Sebastian is the least of our worries," Bella says. "Or did you forget where we are right now?"

"Just tell him you got detention." Eugene shrugs. "Happens to the best of us."

38

Dee bites her lip. "But what if he asks why? I'm not so great at lying to him."

"Dee," Charlie says. "No offense, but if you're going to start spending time with a human, you'll have to get used to lying."

The group hears a squawk in the distance, coming from the corridor. "Shh!" Bella says. "They're coming."

The other three rush to sit down on the bench. A moment later the door opens and Argus swoops inside, then lands gracefully on his perch behind the desk. Principal Koffin moves swiftly into the room behind him.

"Dee Maleficent," she says as she takes a seat. She looks and sounds burned out. "Haven't you had enough punishment for one day?"

"Yes," Dee says. "As a matter of fact, I have. Which raises the question, do I really *need* to be punished again?"

On a normal day such a tongue-in-cheek remark might have garnered a small smile from the principal, but today her face remains as cold and hard as stone.

"Well, let's see." The principal rests her hands on the desk, interlocking her long, slender fingers to emphasize her sharp talons. "Passing magical notes, was it? Is such an activity not against the rules during class?"

Dee fidgets in her seat. "Well, yes, it is. But—"

"And were you not warned by Professor Belinda on the first day of school that getting caught passing notes during class would result in immediate disciplinary action?"

"Yes," Dee says again. "I was."

"*And* were your friends here not *also* aware of the repercussions of magical note passing during class?"

Dee glances at her friends. "Yes, they were."

"So, Dee. You tell me." The principal leans forward in her seat, her gaze piercing. "Do *you* think you deserve to be punished?"

Dee glances over at Bella and drops her voice to a whisper. "A little help here?"

Bella doesn't reply. She sits on her hands and grinds her teeth. She's afraid that if she says one word, her magic will explode. Next to her, Eugene casts his eyes downward, apparently fascinated by a loose thread on his blazer.

Dee sighs and looks back at the principal. "This feels like a trick question."

Charlie puts a cold hand on Dee's shoulder. "We're really sorry, Principal Koffin," they say. "We knew it was against the rules to pass magical notes, but we did it anyway. We deserve whatever punishment you think is fair."

Bella looks at Charlie in disbelief. "You Benedict Arnold!"

Dee frowns. "Who?"

"Perhaps if you spent less time passing notes and more time paying attention in Humans 101," Principal Koffin says irritably, "you would know."

"I pass notes *and* pay attention," Bella pipes in. "Doesn't that count for something?"

Principal Koffin stares blankly at Bella. "No."

Bella slumps in her seat as the principal returns her attention to the group. "Now let's discuss your punishment. . . ."

CHAPTER 4

I was right," Eugene says, frowning down at a filthy cauldron and holding a slimy sponge that's even greener than his hand. "I *would* rather be grounded than doing this."

In addition to extending Dee's detention another day, Principal Koffin looped in the rest of the gang on cauldron-cleaning duty. Even worse, since they were caught passing notes while they were supposed to be learning about humans, Principal Koffin is making them learn how to *clean* like humans instead. Now Bella, Dee, Charlie, and Eugene are each seated at their own table with a basket of sponges and a couple of buckets of soapy water. Professor Daphne snores at her desk, wiped out from her day of rampaging around the grounds.

"But you already *are* grounded," Charlie points out, their voice echoing off the inside of the cauldron as they scrub at a tough stain on the bottom.

"Yeah." Eugene's pointy ears droop a little. "Lucky me."

"Look on the dark side," Dee says, her tone optimistic. "With all four of us cleaning these cauldrons, it won't take nearly as long as it would have if I were here by myself."

Bella laughs, but there is no humor in it. "I'm so glad we could get detention to make your life easier." Some sludge splashes onto her blazer as she scrubs. "Oh, *gross*." With a huff of frustration, she throws the sponge into the cauldron. "We have to do something about Principal Koffin's bad mood."

Dee raises her eyebrows. "What could we do?"

Bella cocks her head, thinking about it. "We could try brewing another Cup of Cheer. We're already in the right place." She gestures to the cauldron in front of her.

"And get in even more trouble?" Dee shakes her head. "I can't handle *another* day of detention."

"Dee's right," Eugene says, putting down his sponge. "And anyway that would only work for a day or so, until the potion wears off. To really cheer her up, we'd have to know what's making her so cranky in the first place."

"Good point," Bella says. She looks around at her friends. "Any ideas?"

They're all quiet for a moment. Then Charlie says, "Maybe it's the weather? I get grumpy when I'm cold too."

"Or maybe she got jury duty," Eugene tries. "That happened to my mom last year, and she was peeved for days."

They all look at Dee to hear her idea. She's hiding behind her cauldron, typing on her eyephone with a smile on her face.

"Dee!" Bella snaps.

"Sorry, sorry." Dee hurries to put her phone away. "But guess what? Sebastian's not mad that I can't make it to the movies! He said we should go together another time instead. Isn't that great?"

"Spook*tacular*," Eugene says in a dry voice. Charlie mumbles their agreement.

Bella's attention stays fixed on her sister, who is blushing and practically bouncing in her seat. Despite all the awful things they've been through today, one text from Sebastian has made Dee positively giddy.

Bella gasps, emitting a burst of yellow sparks from her fingers that makes the light fixture over her desk flicker. "That's it! Maybe

Principal Koffin just needs a little bit of love in her life!"

Dee, Charlie, and Eugene exchange uncertain glances. Nobody says a word.

"Think about it," Bella says, standing up. She starts pacing back and forth. "She's always alone. She's a workaholic. There's no *way* she'd be this grumpy if there was somebody out there sending her cute messages."

Charlie looks at Dee, seeming to understand Bella's train of thought. "You might be onto something," they say. "But what can we do about it? It's not like we can just set her up with someone. . . ."

Their voice trails off when they see the scheming smile forming on Bella's face.

"Oh, no," Dee says. "No! You can't be serious. How would we go about finding a match for the most particular monster in all of Peculiar?"

Bella shrugs. "I don't think it would be that hard."

"Once again I'm going to have to side with

Dee," Eugene says. "We don't really know any-thing about Principal Koffin."

"We know that she's a harpy," Bella says. "We know that she has a passion for education—"

"Eh," Charlie says. "That's debatable."

"We don't know what her type is," Eugene says. "Like, does she like funny people? Tall people? Dead or undead people?"

Bella brushes Eugene's concerns away with a wave of her hand. "We could find all that stuff out."

Eugene seems skeptical. "How?"

"That depends." Bella gives him a mischie-vous look. "How fast can you pick a magic-proof lock on an iron bolt?"

CHAPTER 5

Ten minutes and one half-formed plan later, Bella, Dee, and Eugene sneak out of detention and head west through the empty halls, toward Principal Koffin's tower. Charlie, who firmly believes there is no such thing as *too careful*, elected to stay behind to keep watch over Professor Daphne, lest something happen to rouse her from sleep and they need to explain their friends' absences. Trolls are notoriously deep sleepers, and under the right conditions they can remain in a slumbering state for quite some time. So Charlie found a music playlist on their eyephone called "Peaceful Bedtime Piano," pressed play, and wished their friends good luck.

Bella, Dee, and Eugene arrive at the entrance to the tower stairwell. There is a sign posted on the door, the same sign that pops up every day around this time. It's written in Principal Koffin's careful, slanted script: *Office Closed*.

"What if she's still in there?" Dee says with a worried crease in her brow.

"She's not," Bella assures them. "Every day at three thirty she takes a walk around the grounds, and Argus goes with her. I always see them during scream practice. We're good for at least another half hour."

Bella pushes open the door confidently, and

then abruptly stops. "Well," she sighs. "I didn't see this one coming."

The three friends look up at the long, winding stairwell to find that it's not a stairwell at all but a slide. The steps have been magically flattened down.

"What the . . ." Eugene trails off. He walks up to the flattened stairs and tries to climb them, but immediately loses his footing and slides back to the bottom. "Slippery." He glances back at the twins. "I'll bet she does this whenever her office is closed."

Bella remembers what Charlie said earlier, about the stairway being built to prevent enemies from breaking into the tower. Despite the risk of what they're doing, Bella gets a little excited, curiosity tingling in her belly. What could Principal Koffin be hiding in there?

"We'll have to fly to the top," Bella says. She looks at Dee. "Did you bring your broom? I left mine in my bag."

Dee reaches into her blazer pocket and pulls out a tiny, palm-sized broom. She taps it once, and in a burst of pink sparks, it grows to its full size. She looks up. "I can probably only fit one of you at a time."

"Take Eugene first," Bella says. "He can get started on the lock."

"You got it, Maleficents," he says with a salute. Then he climbs onto the back of Dee's broom. "Uh, just out of curiosity, have you ever flown anyone on this thing before?"

"Nope," Dee says with a grin. "Hang on tight. It might be a bumpy ride."

With jerky, bumblebee-like movements, Dee flies Eugene up to the top of the tower. He hops off the broom onto the landing, rubbing his head in the spot that bonked the wall about twenty feet below.

"Sorry!" Dee says, flying back down to pick up Bella. By the time the twins arrive at the top, Eugene has finished picking the lock and is sitting on the floor, scrolling on his eyephone.

"Just once I'd like a challenge," he says, then pockets his phone and stands up.

The heavy satin curtains are drawn inside Principal Koffin's office, shrouding the room in a still, silent darkness. Dee lets out a small sigh of relief. Until this moment she was convinced the principal would be at her desk, waiting to catch them.

Eugene moves to take a step toward the light switch, but Bella reaches out a hand to stop him. "Wait," she says. "There might be some sort of alarm. I have a feeling she didn't stop at the stairs."

Bella extends an arm like she's holding a torch. "Magic," she says, her voice steady and strong, "reveal yourself."

Blue sparks shoot out from her fingertips and form a smooth, controlled flame, illuminating the friends' faces and the area around them. A few moments pass before two thin blue lines appear at floor level across the center of the room, cutting it into four equal parts.

One of them is hardly an inch from Eugene's sneaker. When he realizes, he jumps back.

"I'm guessing we probably shouldn't touch those," he says, ears pointed on high alert.

"Or anything glowing blue," Bella adds, taking in several enchanted objects around the room. One of which, she notices with a satisfied smirk, is the light switch. What would her friends do without her?

"Dee, some light?" Bella says. "I have to keep hold of this flame, or else the magic markers will disappear."

Dee holds her hands slightly apart in front of her, palms facing each other, and focuses very hard on the space between them. Conjuring pure light, which is different from flames, is one of the most difficult and dangerous spells for a witch to master. When a witch masters the light, she has as much power as the moon itself. She can illuminate the world or plunge it into darkness.

A bead of sweat forms on Dee's brow as she

conjures a ball of light no bigger than a marble. Before it can fizzle out, she sends it shooting toward the antique lamp on Principal Koffin's desk. It lands in the bulb, and the lamp lights up.

"Nice!" Bella says, impressed by her sister's control.

Dee wipes the sweat from her forehead and grins, feeling drained but proud of herself.

Eugene takes a careful step to his right, over the blue line. "Okay, so what exactly are we looking for here? I doubt Koffin keeps a diary where she gushes over crushes."

"Anything personal." Bella's eyes sweep the room. "Anything that tells us about who she is, or what she likes."

"Easier said than done." Eugene looks warily at a tall glass cabinet full of crystals, talismans, and other magical objects. "This place is like a museum."

"Literally," Dee agrees. "Everything in here seems at least a hundred years old." She approaches the wall of dusty-looking leather-bound books and leans forward to read the spines. *"Sixteenth-Century Astronomy. Seventeenth-Century Herbal Medicine. Bird Feeders: A Comprehensive Guide."* Dee scrunches up her nose. "Boring."

"Okay, so she likes history," Bella says. "That means she would probably want to be with someone who's been around for a while, so they can swap stories."

"And she likes reading," Eugene says, gesturing to the wall of books. "I mean, obviously."

"Look." Dee spots a small book resting horizontally on top of several others on the shelf. "A book from this century." She holds it up: *Eddie Gory's Bloody Good Book of Jokes.*

"Ha!" Eugene says. "So she's into humor. Kind of ironic, considering I don't think she's ever laughed a day in her life."

Bella, examining an old tea set, simply shrugs. "Everybody wants to be with someone who can make them laugh."

"Really?" Eugene says, raising an eyebrow.

"Hey, have you ever wondered why the broom was late for work?"

Bella pretends to consider. "Hmm . . . no, definitely not."

"It overswept!" Eugene bursts into laughter. "Get it?"

Bella just shakes her head, but Dee giggles as she makes her way from the bookcase toward Principal Koffin's desk. She glances over the belongings scattered on top. There are some folders, a set of quills, an old-timey pair of glasses. Dee pushes the glasses aside and reads the handwritten letter resting underneath.

"What's that?" Bella asks.

"It's from Principal Oswald Pleasant." Dee skims the note. "He wants YIKESSS and PPS to have another joint event later in the year, after he returns from a . . . what's a 'sabbatical'?"

"Not that," Bella says. "I mean that glowing thing."

She points at a leather-bound book on the far side of the desk, haloed in a forbidding blue glow. Dee leans in to get a closer look but doesn't dare touch it. "It's got her initials on it," she says. "Maybe a day planner?"

"You know, none of this stuff is very personal," Eugene says. He's inspecting what appears to be a sliver of shattered witch glass. "Like, there are no pictures anywhere in here. It's as if she doesn't have any friends or family."

"Maybe she doesn't," Bella says. "When was the last time you saw her hanging out with a friend? When have you even seen her off school grounds?"

"Actually, there is one picture." Dee points at a small portrait hanging on the wall behind the principal's desk, one she noticed earlier but didn't pay much attention to. Strangely, it also glows blue.

"Who would want to steal this?" Bella asks, coming closer. It's a medieval-style painting of three women, a man, and a dog. The women are all tall and severe and dressed in black, with shimmering wings tucked tightly behind their backs. They are all harpies, Bella realizes. She has never seen another harpy besides Principal Koffin before.

Her eyes travel to the center of the photo, where the man sits on a golden throne. His hair is so bright and wild that it looks like fire. He has one hand resting on the dog's head.

"Is that ...," Dee says, pointing at the woman on the far left.

"Principal Koffin," Bella replies, eyes wide. In the portrait she looks a little younger, and her hair hangs down loosely to her waist, but otherwise she's the same. "Who are the other two?"

Dee takes a step closer to get a better look and accidentally trips over a leg of the desk chair. She almost falls directly into the painting but catches herself just in time.

"Phew," she says. "That was a close one."

Bella gasps. "Dee!" She points downward. "Your foot!"

Dee looks down to find that in the process of

catching her balance, she stumbled right across a blue line.

"Eugene," Bella snaps. "Put that ancient relic down. We've got to get out of here."

Eugene puts the Walkman he's holding back where he found it and hurries toward the door. He throws it open, preparing to dive headfirst into the slide-stairs, but stops himself just in time.

"Uh-oh," he says, because the slide has sprouted big spikes, transforming once again. "Guess we're flying down."

Dee pulls her broom from her pocket and zaps it to its full size. There's no time now to worry about whether it can support everyone at once. "Everybody, on!" she says as she mounts. Bella and Eugene both climb onto the back and hold on tight, and Dee propels them off the railing. They fall, swift and hard, but just before they reach the bottom, Dee manages to gain control of the broom and stick the landing.

"Wicked," Eugene says, his balance a little

wobbly as he dismounts. "You know, for a second there I thought we were all going to die."

"We can worry about death later," Bella says. "We need to get back to detention."

They hurry out of the stairwell and across the main corridor, where they turn down a hallway and run, for the second time that day, right into their vice principal—quite literally *into* him this time, as he is a ghost.

"Good heavens!" Vice Principal Archaic says, picking up the book he dropped and adjusting his top hat. "You got *me* this time. Well done."

"We weren't trying to scare you," Dee says, and then immediately regrets it.

"Oh?" the vice principal says. "Where are you students off to in such a rush?"

"Uh . . ." Bella racks her brain for an excuse. "Bathroom. It's *urgent*."

The vice principal raises one skeptical bushy brow. "All three of you?"

Bella, Dee, and Eugene all nod in unison. "We

had the stew for lunch," Bella explains further. "They don't call it *radioactive* for nothing."

Augustus makes a sympathetic face. "Quite right." He nods and steps out of their way. "Well, carry on. And do try to be mindful of other ghosts on your journey, hmm? We aren't as corporeal as everyone else, but we're still here!"

As he turns to go, Bella gets a good look at the book he's holding: *Birds of the Americas*. Dee and Eugene continue down the hall, but she stays put.

Dee and Eugene stop running when they realize Bella isn't with them.

"Bella!" Dee whisper-shouts from down the hall. "What are you doing? We're going to get caught!"

Bella zaps herself to where they're standing. "Vice Principal Archaic! He's the one!"

"Wow," Dee says, amazed at how easily her sister just carried out a Level 5 traveling spell. "Since when can you beam?"

"I've been practicing." Bella runs a casual

hand through her hair. The group starts moving again. "Anyway, Archaic."

Eugene makes a face. "That Monopoly man? No way Koffin will go for it."

"*Eugene*," Dee chides. "That's not a very nice thing to say."

"He's not a Monopoly man," Bella interjects as they turn a corner. "He just wears old clothes. But that's perfect for Principal Koffin, because she likes history, and Archaic is older than time itself. They'll have *lots* to talk about."

"He's got that Monopoly man hat," Eugene mutters, putting a flat hand above his head and raising it up to indicate great height. "We'll have to get rid of that."

"It's not a bad idea," Dee says, ignoring him. "I mean, if Principal Koffin wants someone who likes to joke around, there's nobody better."

"Plus, they both love birds!" Bella adds, getting excited now. "It's perfect!"

"Okay, okay. I see your point," Eugene admits. "So how do we make it happen?"

They return to the Potions classroom to find the door closed. As quietly as she can, Bella opens it a crack to see Professor Daphne still asleep at her desk, snoring loudly to soothing piano sounds. She opens the door all the way, and then she and the others tiptoe inside.

"Looks like Charlie's plan worked well," Eugene says, pausing at the front of the classroom.

"A little too well," Bella agrees. The three friends look at Charlie, who has their head on the table and is fast asleep.

CHAPTER 6

Bella and Dee are standing at their lockers in the witch wing the next morning when Principal Koffin passes by, looking frazzled. Dee, rummaging through her books to find the Supernatural Cultures homework she misplaced, doesn't notice, but Bella seizes the opportunity. She zaps her locker shut and hurries to fall into step with the principal.

"Wicked morning, Principal Koffin," Bella says, hurrying to keep up. "How are things?"

"Horrible, if you must know," the principal says, facing straight ahead. From this angle it's easy for Bella to see the dark circles around her eyes. "Someone broke into my office yesterday after school."

"Oh." Bella puts a hand over her mouth, feigning surprise. "That *is* horrible. Do you know who it was?"

"That remains to be seen." She shoots Bella a suspicious glance. "I don't suppose *you* have any idea who it might have been?"

"What? Me?" Bella forces out a laugh to conceal her pounding heart. "I don't know a thing."

"Perhaps you saw someone hanging around the corridor after school hours?" the principal presses.

Bella shakes her head firmly. "I didn't see

anyone. I was scrubbing cauldrons, remember?"

Principal Koffin doesn't reply. As she turns a corner into the fae wing, she quickens her pace even more.

"So listen," Bella says, practically running now. "I was talking to Vice Principal Archaic earlier, and he told me that he thinks you're the *creepiest*."

The principal's face doesn't change. "Is that so."

"It *is* so!" Bella says. She swerves to narrowly avoid a fairy flying toward her. "The creepiest monster he's ever met—that's what he said."

"Hmm" is the principal's only reply.

"He really respects you," Bella continues. "And Argus, too. He *loves* birds. In fact—"

"Miss Maleficent." Principal Koffin stops walking. "I'm terribly busy. I suggest you make your way to Professor Belinda's classroom now. The homeroom ravens are about to caw."

Instead of waiting for a response, Principal Koffin ruffles her wings and continues on, leaving Bella standing alone in the middle of the hallway.

A smile forms on her face as she watches the principal walk away. *It's a start!*

When she returns to the lockers, she finds that Dee has emptied her entire bag onto the floor and is frantically searching through its contents. "I can't find my homework anywhere. I think Cornelius might've been sleeping on it this morning."

Bella shakes her head. "That cat will sleep anywhere besides his bed." She points a finger in the air and casts a retrieving spell. A few seconds later a worksheet appears in Dee's hands.

Dee smiles, then blows some stray cat hairs off the paper. "I *knew* it." She looks at her sister. "Since when can you do that?"

Bella waves a hand like it was nothing. "I checked out some advanced-spell books from the library. No big deal."

In homeroom Bella, Dee, Charlie, and Eugene huddle together at their desks.

"How did it go with Koffin?" Eugene asks. "Is she in love with Archaic yet?"

"Not exactly," Bella admits. "She basically ignored me when I tried talking to her."

"Same with Gus," Charlie says. "We did what you said—we told him Principal K thinks he's creepy and suggested he should ask her on a date, and he got all nervous and disappeared."

Dee rests her elbows on her desk and puts her chin in her hands. "I never would've thought someone who loves scaring so much could be frightened off by a little romance," she says. Unwittingly her eyes flick to Bella.

Bella exhales quickly and decisively. "Well, we're just going to have to try harder." She looks around at her friends. "Are we ready for phase two?"

Eugene raises his eyebrows. "Phase two?"

Bella nods once. "Operation Get Archaic and Koffin Together, No Matter the Cost."

"Operation *GAKTNMC*?" Charlie recites, frowning. "Doesn't exactly have a ring to it."

The group considers for a moment. Then Dee says, "How about 'Operation Love Spell'?"

Bella, Charlie, and Eugene exchange a look, and then everyone nods their agreement.

"Okay," Bella says, putting her hand in the center of the huddle. "To Operation Love Spell."

The others add their hands to the pile. "Operation Love Spell," they all echo.

The first mission is assigned to Dee, who takes a detour to Principal Koffin's office on her way to class. She cuts across the main corridor and slips through the entrance at the bottom of the tower. Pausing at the foot of the winding staircase—which has returned to its usual, steplike form—she removes her tiny broom from one pocket and an even tinier bouquet of black roses from the other. Bella plucked them from their dads' garden this morning and then shrank them with magic. "To Yvette. Love, Gus," she said with a pleased grin.

Dee zaps the broom and the flowers to their full size and flies to the landing at the top of the stairs. She places the bouquet in front of Principal Koffin's door, adjusting the stems until the roses are arranged nicely, and then gives the door two swift knocks. As fast as she can, she jumps over the edge of the landing with her broom and hides beneath the stairs, hovering in the air.

She hears Principal Koffin open the door. A few moments pass. Then Dee hears the principal say, "Gretchen?"

The heavy clacking sound of high heels approaches the landing, followed by a voice. "Well, well, what do we have here?"

Dee claps a hand over her mouth. She'd recognize Gretchen Cauldronson's snooty, high-pitched voice anywhere.

"I'm not sure," the principal says, her voice taut, maybe even a little distressed.

Gretchen speaks again. "Do you think these flowers have anything to do with—"

"*Shh,*" Yvette hisses, cutting her off. "Anyone could be lurking. Do me a favor and incinerate them."

Dee hears a *whoosh*, followed by the smell of smoke and the sound of a slammed door. She hears the locks in the door click, then waits a few moments in silence before peeking over the edge of the landing.

The roses are on the floor, reduced to a crispy pile of ashes.

Dee winces. Maybe she should've added a note.

Meanwhile Charlie stands outside the vice principal's office, taking a few deep breaths for courage. When they work up the nerve, they pull an envelope out of their blazer pocket with the words *From your secret admirer* printed on the outside, enchanted by Bella to mimic Yvette's careful writing. They place it right outside the door and hurry away.

A few moments later the door opens, and out steps Eugene with the vice principal. Only, he doesn't quite look like the vice principal. Gone is his top hat, revealing a shockingly full head of wavy brown hair, and he wears a fashionable sport coat and tapered trousers that appear to be from this century. From this *decade*, even.

"Are you sure I don't look foolish?" Augustus says, self-consciously touching the top of his head, then his freshly shaved face. "I haven't gone without my mustache since Lincoln was in office. And I feel so . . . underdressed."

"What did I tell you?" Eugene says. "It's going to be so much easier to scare people if you blend in with them. You've got the element of surprise on your side now."

The vice principal nods. "I suppose I can't argue with you there." He looks down at his outfit. "I certainly won't miss that blasted cummerbund." Then he notices the note on the floor. "Hmm, what's this?"

He bends over to pick it up. When he recognizes the handwriting, his face immediately goes two shades paler.

"What is it, Mr. A?" Eugene peeks over the vice principal's shoulder, feigning interest.

Augustus tucks the note into his coat pocket. "Nothing to concern yourself with, Eugene. I think it's time you head back to class."

"Sure thing, big A," Eugene says with a dramatic wink. "By the way, can I get an—"

The vice principal retreats into his office and slams the door.

Eugene's ears droop. "Excuse slip?"

When the clock strikes twelve, all four friends, located in various wings around the school, put in their blueteeth to regroup.

What's everyone's progress? Bella thinks from a bathroom stall in the witch wing.

Charlie, returning to their Compulsion class in the vampire wing, is the first to reply. *Archaic got the note, but he still hasn't left his office. I just did another walk-by.*

He's probably waiting for the right time to ask Koffin out, Eugene thinks, slouching into his desk in Supernatural Cultures. *Don't worry, Maleficent. The makeover I gave him is so good, there's no way she'll be able to resist him.*

Excellent. Bella smiles. *Dee, did Koffin like the flowers?*

NO. Dee's thoughts come through like a shout. *SHE BURNED THEM.*

What do you mean, she burned them? Charlie thinks.

And why are you yelling? Eugene adds.

I'M A LITTLE BUSY AT THE MOMENT, Dee replies. *I'M TRYING NOT TO GET HIT WITH A CREAM PIE.*

We're doing UFO drills in Met Ed today, Bella explains to Charlie and Eugene. Once a week their Metaphysical Education teacher makes them mount their brooms and dodge whatever object she feels like throwing at them, so they can practice agility. Today that object is cream pies. It's why Bella is hiding in the bathroom. *Dee, remember to relax your grip! The broom can sense your fear.*

Once again Charlie asks, *Why did Principal Koffin burn the flowers?*

SHE DIDN'T KNOW THEY WERE FROM

ARCHAIC, Dee thinks. *SHE WAS—AH, MY SHOE—SUSPICIOUS.*

Bella groans. It feels like they're getting nowhere. *Okay,* she thinks as she emerges from the stall. *We need a new plan, stat. Dee, I'll meet you in the locker room.*

With missions one through three of Operation Love Spell complete but yielding little in the way of results, a frustrated Bella decides she can't wait around for fate to bring the principal and vice principal together—she'll have to do it herself.

At the beginning of lunch, Bella eagerly takes off in the direction of Principal Koffin's office, while Dee, slightly *less* eager because the mission is cutting into her favorite time of day, sets out to locate the vice principal.

Bella finds Yvette first, crossing the main corridor. "Principal Koffin!" she calls out from some distance away, urgently waving her arms. "Come quick!"

The principal lets out an irritated sigh that echoes off the walls. "What *now*?"

"Someone accidentally created a portal to another dimension in the botanical wing!"

The principal's eyes momentarily widen with alarm, and then narrow skeptically. "By 'someone' do you mean yourself?"

Bella shakes her head vigorously. "I was on my way to the cafeteria when I saw it. Room 314. I think someone is trapped in there!"

Principal Koffin hesitates for a moment, like she's unsure whether to believe Bella. Then she decisively flaps her wings and takes off in the direction of the botanical wing. Bella runs after her, pumping her legs as fast as she can to keep up.

On the other side of the school, Dee finds the vice principal in his office, reading and rereading one single page of creased paper. When he sees Dee coming, he hurries to fold the paper up and shove it into his desk drawer.

"Dee Maleficent," he says by way of greeting. When he gets a closer look at her face, his forehead creases with concern. "What's the matter?"

"There's a black hole in the botanical wing!" she says, and then backtracks, forgetting this part of the plan. "Er—wait. It might also be a portal to another dimension? I forget."

Without any hesitation the vice principal gets up from his desk and hurries out of the office, blurring his corporeal form to float as fast as he can toward the scene.

"Oh, room 314!" Dee calls out after him.

Principal Koffin is the first to arrive at the classroom, rushing through the doorway and frantically looking around for any signs of an interdimensional portal. Vice Principal Archaic arrives a few moments later.

"Yvette!" he says. When he sees her, his skin gets a little more transparent—the ghostly equivalent of blushing. "Did—did you already remove the black hole?"

"Black hole?" She looks suspicious. "I was

told it was a portal." Then, seeming to notice him for the first time, she looks him up and down. "Augustus," she says, taken aback. "Your clothes."

Before he can respond, the classroom door shuts and locks behind him. He glances at the door, and then back at Principal Koffin. "Did you do that?"

Bella snickers into her hands on the other side of the wall, just out of view.

"Now they'll *have* to fall in love!" she whispers to Dee, who just arrived and is still panting from running all over the school. "Did you see the way she looked at him? It's *just* like Helena and Alistair."

"I guess," Dee says. "Besides the fact that Alistair kicked Helena off the show."

Suddenly the door bursts off its hinges and into the hallway with a heavy gust of wind. Bella rushes to take cover, while a frightened Dee can't help but scream.

Principal Koffin relaxes her wings as she

steps through the doorway. When she sees the twins, she raises her wings back to their full, intimidating height.

"You two!" she roars, angrier than the twins have ever seen her. "I should have known. *What* is the meaning of this?"

"Um . . ." Dee laughs nervously. "I guess the portal fixed itself?"

The principal puts her hands on her hips and glowers down at the girls. Bella and Dee inch closer together, bracing themselves for the worst.

"Your antics this week have been entirely unacceptable," she says. "You've given me no choice but to—"

Vice Principal Archaic appears behind her and taps her on the shoulder. "Excuse me, Yvette?"

She shoots him an irritated glance. "Not now, Augustus."

"I apologize for my most untimely interruption, but I've got to get down to the cafeteria for lunch monitor duty," he says. "I was just wondering if . . . if perhaps you'd like to accompany me to lunch sometime?"

The twins let out gasps of delight, while Principal Koffin blinks in surprise.

"There's this quaint little sandwich shop just outside of town," the vice principal continues, talking through his nerves. "Perhaps we could—"

The principal's face hardens. "No," she says, turning up her nose. "I'm afraid I can't."

"What?" Bella whines. "But, Principal Koffin—"

"Enough," the principal snaps. She turns to Vice Principal Archaic, who has all but sunk into the wall of lockers with embarrassment. She softens her tone just a little. "I'm sorry, Augustus, but it would be impossible."

"Not to worry," he says, and lets out a discomfited little laugh. "Not to worry. I'll just . . .

erm, I had best be off." He floats away as quickly as he can, without another word.

Principal Koffin watches him go for a moment, still a little stunned, and then composes herself. She turns the full weight of her fury back on to Bella and Dee. "Now, where was I?"

CHAPTER 7

Thiis is so unfair," Bella grumbles into the cauldron she's scrubbing. "We try to do something nice for Principal Koffin, and this is how she repays us? With *more* detention?"

Bella and Dee are in their Potions classroom, cleaning cauldrons after school for the second day in a row. Professor Daphne, acting once again as their detention monitor, sleeps soundly at her desk, not to be disturbed, no matter how many times Dee accidentally sends a sudsy cauldron crashing to the floor.

"She wasn't nice to Vice Principal Archaic, either," Dee says as she squeezes her sponge over a bucket. "Poor guy. Did you see how sad he looked?"

Bella recalls the crushed expression on Archaic's face when Principal Koffin refused him—just like Helena when Alistair gave his broom to Serafina on Monday's episode of *Which Witch Is the One*? "Yeah. She could've at least come up with an excuse, instead of just saying no." Bella channels her frustration into her sponge by squeezing and scrubbing harder. "And what did she mean by 'it would be impossible,' anyway? What's impossible about lunch?"

"Take a breath, Bella," Dee warns. "Or else you'll zap that cauldron to smithereens."

"I'm just *saying*." Bella continues scrubbing. "Operation Love Spell worked perfectly on Vice

Principal Archaic. What's Principal Koffin's problem? Why is she *so* against falling in love?"

Red sparks sizzle on Bella's fingertips, and the cauldron cracks beneath her hands. She groans. Fortunately, Professor Daphne is unfazed, still snoring softly at her desk.

Dee shrugs. "Maybe she's not against it. Maybe it's just a little harder for her." She feels her eyephone buzz in her pocket and blushes, guessing who it might be without having to look.

"What do you mean?" Bella zaps the broken cauldron pieces into a nearby trash can and then crosses her arms. "And why is your face all red?"

Dee puts a hand to her cheek self-consciously. "I mean . . . we don't know what she's been through. Maybe something happened in her past that made her put walls up." She picks up her sponge and gets to work on a new cauldron. "Maybe she's had her heart broken. Like Helena."

The anger falls from Bella's face as she considers this. "Jeepers creepers, it *is* just like Helena and Alistair. She still had walls up from her last relationship, so Alistair couldn't get close to her, and that's why he sent her home!"

Dee raises an eyebrow. "What's your point?"

"My point," Bella says, dropping her sponge, "is that Principal Koffin will never be able to fall in love if she keeps her walls up. We have to help her!"

"Right," Dee says, her voice flat. She's resisting the urge to check her eyephone notifications. "I thought that was what we've been doing all day today with Operation Love Spell."

"But there's one thing we still haven't tried." Bella's eyes brighten. "A love spell!"

Now Dee drops her sponge too. "*No.* Or are you trying to turn our detention into an expulsion?"

"But why not?" Bella presses. "We've got everything we could possibly need to cast the spell right here." She gestures to the supply closet of ingredients at the back of the room. "We could do it fast."

Dee glances at Professor Daphne. "We can't perform a love spell while she's sleeping right there. What if she wakes up?"

"She's not going to wake up," Bella assures her sister. "See?" She picks up the cauldron she just started cleaning and throws it down onto the floor so that it shatters. Professor Daphne doesn't stir.

Dee bites her lip and says nothing.

"Dee, come *on*," Bella begs. "If we don't do this, Professor Koffin could stay in this bad mood forever, and who knows how many more detentions we'll get?" She looks at the broken cauldron pieces by her feet and zaps those into the trash with the others. "I *can't* clean any more cauldrons. I'll lose my mind."

Dee looks down at her hands. She wants Principal Koffin to cheer up just as much as Bella does. She certainly doesn't want any more detention. But how can they guarantee that this spell will do the trick?

"Okay," Dee says. She feels her phone buzz in her pocket again. "But we have to be as specific as possible. We can't leave any room for loopholes."

"I'm with you." Bella gets her Level 1 Spell Casting handbook out of her book bag and uses magic to flip through its pages. "I'm pretty sure there's nothing in here that will help us." She pauses on page 102, which includes a charm for attracting woodland creatures, and then slams the book closed. "*Ugh.* We need a higher-level casting book."

"How are we going to get one of those?" Dee asks.

Bella shakes her head. "We can't. At least not right now." Then her gaze lands on a set of shelves across the room, where about two dozen Potions textbooks, Levels 1 through 5, sit unattended. A wicked smile spreads across her face. "But I'll bet we can find something in there."

Dee bites her thumbnail, feeling uncertain. "Are you sure this is a good idea? I can barely brew a Level One potion."

"Oh, it will be fine," Bella says, already moving toward the books. "I've been doing a lot of extra reading lately, remember?"

Approximately forty-three snores from Professor Daphne later, Bella finds a recipe for a Potion of Vulnerability in the *Love Spells* section of a Level 3 Potions book. "'A potion for letting down one's defenses to reveal the truth of the heart within,'" Bella reads. She looks up at Dee. "That seems like it could do the trick. What do you think?"

"Yeah," Dee says, her eyes on her phone and her fingers flying across the keypad. She and Sebastian are planning another trip to the movies. "Totally."

Bella narrows her eyes. "Did you even hear what I said?"

"*Yes,*" Dee says, though really she only heard about half of it. She puts her phone

89

away and looks at Bella. "Potion of Vulnerability. Let's do it."

Bella conjures a flame beneath a cauldron at the back of the room while Dee gathers the necessary supplies. She lists the ingredients as she places them on the table. "St. John's wort, crushed rose petals, moondust, and eggshell. The only thing missing is fresh tears." She looks at Bella. "How are we going to get those?"

Without taking her eyes off the flame, Bella holds one hand up in the air and zaps an onion from their pantry at home into her palm. Dee looks at it, confused. Then the onion starts peeling itself, and almost as quickly, Dee's eyes begin to water.

"Hey!" Dee scolds, putting her hands over her eyes.

"Sorry," Bella says, a guilty look on her face. "Quick, grab a vial and catch some tears while you're still crying."

With the last ingredient secured, Bella and Dee get to work brewing the potion, following the directions as carefully as they can. By the time they get to the last step, when everything is boiling in the cauldron, they're both sweating, and the steam has frizzed up their hair.

Dee looks down at the textbook. "It says we have to say an incantation into the cauldron," she reads. "So the potion can absorb its 'true purpose.'" She puts the last bit in air quotes.

"What kind of incantation?" Bella asks, stoking the flame with her sparks.

Dee makes a face as she skims the page. "Doesn't say. I think you're just supposed to tell it what you want it to do."

"Okay, then." Bella stares down into the honey-colored liquid boiling inside the cauldron. "Potion, please make Principal Koffin let down her walls—"

"No, not like that," Dee says. "Like an incantation. Give it *rhythm*."

Bella takes a deep breath. She looks into the potion and tries again.

"Yvette Koffin," Bella whispers. "Let down

your walls so your vulnerability shines through, and you'll find a love that's strong and true."

She looks up at Dee, who shrugs and says, "Seems good enough to me."

Bella nods, satisfied. "Okay. All we have to do now is let it brew for ten minutes. Then we sprinkle a little bit on her doorknob, and voilà!" She claps her hands together in excitement. "As soon as she touches it, the potion will seep into her skin, and Operation Love Spell will officially be a success."

The girls both look down into the potion, which swirls and sparkles like liquid gold. Then they look at each other and smile.

CHAPTER 8

Bella and Dee enter homeroom the next day in high spirits. When they sit down at their desks, looking confident and relaxed, Eugene and Charlie swap a puzzled glance.

"You witches are surprisingly calm this morning," Eugene says. He looks at Bella.

"Especially you. I would've thought you'd be on the warpath after two days of detention."

Bella shrugs and starts fiddling with her hair. "Principal Koffin's bad mood is yesterday's news. I have a feeling that today things will be different."

"Really?" Eugene leans forward in his seat. "What did you do?"

"Nothing against the rules, I hope," Charlie says, not looking up from the homework they're rushing to finish.

Bella's smile is small and smug. "Let's just say we got her to let down her walls." Behind Bella, Dee giggles into her *Howler* comic.

"Sounds like it was against the rules," Eugene mutters to Charlie, who nods in agreement.

"Speaking of letting down walls," Charlie says. "Did you hear about the pixie-dust spill?"

Dee's jaw drops. "The *what*?"

The raven in the corner caws to signal the start of the morning announcements. "Quiet, everyone!" Professor Belinda calls out from her desk. She's slumped forward, clearly exhausted. Before the twins have time to wonder why, Principal Koffin's voice echoes through the raven, and the intensity behind it sends a shiver down every spine in the room.

"Students and faculty, listen up, *now*," the principal snarls, and Bella winces. That's certainly not the way someone who's madly in love is *supposed* to sound.

"I have some distressing news. In the early hours of this morning, the fae wing had a security breach. The vault containing our school's entire supply of pixie dust was broken open, causing a major leak."

Bella widens her eyes. Without a fairy to control it, pixie dust is pure chaos magic. A leak in the school would mean halls turning into mazes, lockers that move and change, erupting candle fire—anything to sow fear and confusion. As far as she knows, a leak like this has never happened at YIKESS before.

"Luckily," the principal continues, "we were able to contain the dust and repair the vault before any major damage was done. *Unluckily*, that doesn't change the fact that someone deliberately tried to wreak havoc on school grounds, effectively putting all of you in danger."

Murmurs spread across the classroom. Was it a prank gone wrong? An accident? It couldn't *possibly* be a real intruder, could it?

As the principal continues, her voice gets even more grim. "Were this an isolated incident, I would be less concerned; I'd perhaps even chalk it up to some misguided young monster looking to cause a stir. However, this leak comes on the heels of another concerning event. Two days ago my office was broken into after school hours, and the culprit still has not been found."

Bella looks around at her friends, who are all wearing the same panicked expressions. When Dee meets her eye, Bella knows they're thinking the same thing. *We are* so *getting into trouble*.

"Your safety is my top concern," Principal

Koffin says. "Therefore, I have no choice but to cancel next week's Harvest Moon Feast, and any other YIKESSS events moving forward that could put you in harm's way, until whoever is responsible comes forward."

The class lets out a collective groan, Eugene loudest of all. The Harvest Moon Feast is the supernatural equivalent of a Thanksgiving feast for humans, and Eugene was looking forward to setting the record for most cauldron cakes eaten in a single night.

"In the meantime it's important that you all stay vigilant," the principal continues. "If you see something suspicious, it is your *responsibility* to tell someone."

She hesitates, as if debating whether to say more. Finally she says, "That's all for today." The raven closes its mouth, and she's gone.

"We didn't do it!" Dee says, quickly closing her comic book. "Right?"

"We *did* break into her office," Charlie points out, clearly worried.

"*Shh!*" Bella hisses at them to be quiet. "That doesn't have anything to do with the pixie-dust leak. They're two separate incidents that just *happened* to take place two days apart." She shrugs. "It could happen to anyone."

"Hey." Eugene grins. "Whoever broke into the vault of pixie dust will probably get blamed for breaking into her office, too, right? Then we'll be off the hook."

"Or *maybe* whoever broke into her office will also get blamed for the pixie dust," Dee says with a concerned crease in her brow. "I can't get another day of detention! My hands are starting to prune from all the cauldron scrubbing."

"Don't worry, Dee." Bella keeps her voice low. "Eugene's right. We just have to make sure whoever leaked the pixie dust gets caught first."

Charlie sighs. "And *how* are we supposed to do that?"

"By keeping our eyes open," Bella says. "And our heads down."

Charlie puts their head on the desk and mumbles into their worksheet. "Why can't we ever just have a normal day at school?"

When Bella, Dee, Charlie, and Eugene leave for their first classes, they're on the lookout for even the smallest signs of trouble. As it turns out, the group doesn't need to look for very long. They're all only a few steps out the door when they hear screaming in the distance, coming from the direction of the botanical wing.

"Those don't sound like shrieking sunflowers to me," Eugene says, his ears perking up. He looks at Bella. "What do you say, Maleficent?"

Bella doesn't hesitate. "Let's go." She turns on her heel and leads the way. As they hurry toward the commotion, they pass crowds of students rushing in the opposite direction.

"Remind me why we're running *toward* what everybody else seems to be running away from?" Charlie says, their voice fraught with worry.

"Aw, c'mon, Charlie," Eugene urges, excitement in his eyes. "We're monsters. Sometimes we've gotta live life on the edge."

"Tell that to my stomach," Charlie says. "It really doesn't care for surprises."

When they get to the botanical wing, they realize the noises are coming from the greenhouse, home to the school's extensive supply of plants, herbs, and flowers. The screaming has stopped, replaced by other strange noises like hissing and growling. The friends pause just outside, unsure of what they might be walking into. Have the magical creatures escaped from the stables somehow? Is Professor Daphne in another one of her moods?

"I have a strange feeling," Dee says. She's not sure how, but she knows that the plants inside the greenhouse are angry. "I don't know if we should go in there."

Bella ignores her and rushes through the door. When she sees what's inside, her jaw drops.

"Jeepers—" she starts but doesn't finish, because a vine extends from out of nowhere and snatches her up.

"Bella!" Dee rushes in after her sister to discover that the entire room has come alive. All around her, plants thrash, writhe, and roar like vicious toddlers throwing a tantrum. She watches Bella scream as she gets tossed around in the air by several tenacious vines as tall and thick as tree trunks. Everything has grown to five or six times its normal size. Some plants have even grown teeth.

"Put me down!" Bella pounds her fists into the vine around her waist and conjures flames, scalding the plant and forcing it to relax its grip as it shrivels back in pain. But it's no use: when one vine drops her, another simply catches her midair. It doesn't take long for her to realize that there are too many vines to fight off this way.

"Don't worry, Bella!" Dee calls out, trying to ignore how very worried *she* is. "We'll find a way to get you down!"

Devil's ivy snakes across the floor nearby, and when Eugene and Charlie follow Dee into the room, they accidentally step on a few leaves. The angry ivy hisses, rears up, wraps itself around Eugene's and Charlie's ankles, and squeezes tight.

"Oh no!" Charlie wails as the ivy creeps up their legs. "They've got me! This is how it ends!"

Eugene shakes his head at Charlie's fear. "Wouldn't you rather die doing something exciting than live a boring life forever?"

"No!" Charlie yanks at the ivy, but it won't budge. "I want to read books in a cozy coffin. That's it."

They're both distracted by Bella's scream as a vine spins her in the air. Eugene winces. "At least we're not up there."

As soon as he says it, the ivy gathers below Eugene's and Charlie's feet and raises them both up to the ceiling. "Oh great," Charlie says, the vines taking over their arms now. "The plants have a sense of humor."

As her friends get lifted above her head, Dee notices a few tiny, shimmering specks of gold raining down from the devil's ivy. She gasps. "It's pixie dust!" Then she says more loudly, so the others can hear, "Somebody used pixie dust to enchant the plants!"

"Does that mean a fairy will be able to—*ouch!*—stop them?" Bella asks, as the vine around her waist squeezes tighter.

"Maybe," Dee replies. "I'd better go get Principal K—" Her sentence gets cut off as a tree branch wraps itself around one of her ankles and then lifts her into the air so that she's dangling upside down. Dee screams.

"Charlie," Bella shouts. "Turn yourself into a bat, and you'll slip out of the ivy!"

Charlie looks anxiously down at the vines creeping across their chest. "I don't know if I can! I'm too nervous."

"Yes, you can!" Eugene says, the ivy tangling across his limbs. "Pretend we're at a flyball game. You have to turn, or else you can't play."

Charlie squeezes their red eyes shut, concentrating. After a few seconds they disappear, then reemerge from the ivy as a small, red-eyed bat.

"I did it!" They smile, and the sun glints off their tiny fangs. They rapidly pump their wings to stay in the air. "Okay, I'll go get help. Hang on!"

Bella snorts, clutching the vine that holds her hostage. "Like I have a choice?"

Across the room Dee struggles to free herself from the twisted branch, only to realize that freeing herself would mean crashing headfirst into the ground. "Tree, put me down! Please!" She looks around for a vine to grab on to, or anything that might be able to help her. That's when she sees it.

In the corner, a smoky shadow of a man, giggling into his hands.

"Poltergeist!" she yells, pointing at the monster.

"Poltergeist?" Bella looks where her sister

points, but the monster is already on the move. Poltergeists are nefarious tricksters whose sole purpose in the afterlife is to cause trouble. When Bella finally spots it, her eyes widen with understanding. "Oh. Well, that explains it."

"But what is it doing *here*?" Eugene asks from the ceiling, the ivy now wrapping up his chest.

Dee purses her lips, thinking. Poltergeists, as well as all other malevolent monsters, are usually kept away from YIKESSS by the protective veil that surrounds the school. Maybe this one found a crack in the foundation somehow?

Suddenly Dee realizes she's once again just a few feet off the ground. She was so busy thinking about the poltergeist that she didn't notice that the tree had listened to her when she'd told it to put her down. The branch relaxes its grip on her ankle, and Dee slides out of it easily.

"Thanks, tree," she says, standing upright. "Um, could you maybe ask your plant friends to let the others go too? They're my friends."

The branch shrinks back toward the trunk of the tree. A few moments pass, and then, slowly, the other plants start to calm down. They lower Bella and Eugene to the ground and unravel their vines.

"Whoa," Dee says. "Who'd have thought that all we needed to do was ask them to let us go?"

Eugene stretches out his limbs while Bella leans forward with her hands on her knees, looking a little green. "I *did*," she says.

"But you didn't ask nicely," Dee recalls. "Plants are living beings too, you know. They probably have feelings."

"Whatever." Eugene pushes a section of ivy aside like a curtain and heads for the door. "Let's just get out of here."

Bella groans. "We're going to be *so* late for class." She stands up and starts to follow him, then changes her mind and leans against a tree trunk. "On second thought maybe I should go to the nurse."

Dee drapes Bella's arm over her shoulders. "I'll take you," she says. "Eugene, you should go catch up with Charlie and tell them the poltergeist is the one who broke into the pixie-dust vault."

"On it," he says, quickening his pace.

"I can't believe you're not more freaked out right now," Bella says to Dee as they move slowly after him.

"Principal Koffin can handle one poltergeist," Dee says, brushing a vine out of her way. "She'll get rid of it, and everything will go back to normal."

"Not about that," Bella says. "I'm talking about the fact that you just told a roomful of enchanted plants what to do, and they *listened*."

"Oh," Dee replies. "Yeah. When you put it like that, I guess it does seem a little unusual."

"A little?"

The girls are interrupted by Principal Koffin and Professor Belinda bursting into the greenhouse.

"Girls," Professor Belinda says, startled to see them. "What are you still doing here? Go, quickly!"

Holding on to each other, Bella and Dee hurry out of the room without another word, the plants bending and shifting to clear a path as they go.

CHAPTER 9

The poltergeist is no match for Principal Koffin and Professor Belinda. As it turns out, they were already on their way to the botanical wing when they bumped—or rather, *flew*—into Charlie, who rushed to fill them in on what had just transpired in the greenhouse. After Bella and Dee make their escape, the principal and professor corral the poltergeist into a corner so that Professor Belinda can zap it back to the ether where it came from.

The twins hope that after the poltergeist is banished, everything will return to normal and Principal Koffin can finally focus on opening her heart to Vice Principal Archaic. Unfortunately, things in Peculiar are rarely so simple. Over the next few days a slew of strange occurrences continues to plague YIKESSS, sending the principal into full-on crisis mode.

More dark creatures show up and start causing trouble: sprite gremlins pick a food fight in the cafeteria, ghouls hide in lockers to steal screams, *another* poltergeist breaks into the Potions supply closet to mix up ingredients. A third-year kelpie even dives into the swimming pool only to be surprised by a horned hydra napping in the deep end.

But the worst comes on Monday morning, when Bella discovers that a video of Friday night's flyball game has been circulating on the internet—not the monsternet but the *human* internet. Apparently, a human out for a walk noticed the shimmering flyball in the distance and decided to climb the hill up to YIKESSS for a closer look. *I had to film this so other people would believe me,* reads the caption on the video post. *And so I would believe my own eyes.* Since it was posted Saturday morning, the video has racked up hundreds of thousands of views.

"How is this possible?" Bella asks, pulling her phone closer to her face to get a better look. The video shows Charlie, in bat form, passing the flyball to their classmate Mildred on her broom, and then the two teams racing to the goalposts, which float in midair. Mildred passes the ball to Drake, who passes back to Charlie, who then uses their wing to smack the ball past the goalie and into the net for five points.

"Nice shot," Dee says to Charlie, watching over Bella's shoulder. Behind her a nervous Charlie smiles into their lap.

"Lucky shot," Crypta mumbles with an eye

roll. Since Professor Belinda is away dealing with the crisis of the hour—a swarm of pesky nettleflies in the metaphysical education wing this time—the entire class has their eyephones out to watch the video.

"She's just jealous," Eugene assures Charlie with a pat on the shoulder. "She knows you're the best, and she *wishes* she could do that."

"Oh yeah," Crypta says. "I *wish* I were exposing our secret to the entire world. You got me."

"Back off, Crypta," Bella snaps, as Charlie sinks lower into their seat. "I'm sure the Creepy Council is already working on fixing it. By tomorrow, I'll bet none of the humans will even remember."

"And it's not Charlie's fault," Dee adds. "Humans aren't supposed to be able to see past the veil."

Charlie considers this and then sits up a little straighter. "Yeah. It's *not* my fault. It's like the veil is malfunctioning or something."

Next to them Eugene nods. "Actually, you've

got a point. All the weird stuff that's been happening lately should be impossible because of the veil."

"And if the veil *did* get knocked down," Charlie continues, "we'd have no way of knowing. We'd just be sitting ducks, vulnerable to whatever comes our way."

Bella turns Charlie's words over in her mind and then widens her eyes. She turns to Dee, who's looking back at her with the same panicked expression.

"You don't think—" Bella begins.

"Is this because of the spell?" Dee finishes her thought.

"A *spell*?" Charlie repeats. Bella and Dee both shush them.

"Oh no," Eugene says. "*What* did you witches do now?"

Bella puts a finger to her lips, motioning for her friends to be quiet. She glances back at Crypta, who is definitely trying to eavesdrop. She lowers her voice and begins twirling her finger through her hair. "Nothing much. We just brewed a little love potion to get Principal Koffin to let down her walls."

"Only, now it kind of seems like the *wall* we let down," Dee says, putting air quotes around "wall," "is the veil of protection." She starts to feel a little sick.

"You know, two months ago my biggest problem was my garlic allergy." Charlie says, shaking their head. "Those were the days."

"Ugh!" Bella groans and throws her hands up. "We should have been more specific!"

"We shouldn't have done a Level Three spell," Dee mutters. All she wanted to do was scrub cauldrons and *occasionally* text Sebastian in peace.

"Oh, *man*." Eugene winces. "And I thought being grounded for a week was bad. You two are going to be grounded *forever*."

"If we're lucky," Dee says in a mopey voice. "I'll probably never see Sebastian again. Not to mention daylight."

Bella shakes her head in disbelief. "That's who you're thinking about right now? Really? With everything going on?"

"What?" Dee blushes. "I can't help it. He's so *cute*."

The raven squawks to signal the end of homeroom, and instead of going to first period, Bella and Dee head straight to Principal Koffin's office to come clean. They take their time climbing the winding staircase, and when they finally arrive at the top, the door is open and the principal is sitting at her desk, writing furiously on a piece of paper. Resting on his perch behind her, Argus the crow lets out a squawk.

"Come in," the principal says without raising her head.

The twins both try to shove the other through the doorway first, and then end up stumbling in at the same time.

"Um, hi, Principal Koffin," Dee says, straightening and plastering a false smile onto her face. "How are you today?"

"Out with it, Donna," the principal says, still not looking at the girls. "I have a nine thirty meeting."

"You *might* want to cancel it," Bella says, almost as an aside. Principal Koffin snaps her head up.

"What's happened now?" The principal puts down her pen and stands. "Another poltergeist?"

"No, no," Dee says, although if their theory is correct, there very well *could* be one lurking somewhere. "But we do think we know what's causing the poltergeists. And the sprite gremlins, and the hydra, and—"

"We accidentally knocked down the veil of protection," Bella blurts out. "At least, we think we did."

The twins brace themselves for outrage, but instead Principal Koffin goes very still. She stands there for a moment like a looming tower over the twins, her face unreadable as she processes what has just been said. Then, slowly, she sits back down. She places her hands on the desk in front of her, crosses her manicured talons, and says, "Tell me everything."

So they do. They tell her about the love potion, all the matchmaking schemes, and the vice principal's makeover. Dee even fesses up to breaking into Principal Koffin's office, though Bella thinks they probably could've left that part out.

When they finish speaking, Principal Koffin doesn't say anything. She stays silent for so long, in fact, that Bella and Dee swap a wary glance.

Finally she looks back at Argus, still and silent on his perch. She says one word: "Belinda." And the bird takes off out the door.

"This is very serious," the principal says, turning back to the girls. "You meddled in affairs that were not your own, with a potion that was much too advanced for you to carry out correctly, and have now managed to undo the work of magic that is centuries old and extremely powerful. Have I missed anything?"

"The fact that we're really sorry?" Dee tries.

"But I don't understand." Bella crosses her arms. "If it's so old and powerful, how did we mess it up with one little spell?"

The principal looks down her nose at Bella. "I once told you both that you have a great power inside you. I still believe this is true. But if you don't have the patience to learn how to control it, then believe me. *It* will control *you*."

In a flash Professor Belinda beams into the center of the room with Argus on her arm. She looks around warily. Leading the hunt against the dark monsters has left her even more exhausted than Principal Koffin.

"Girls? Yvette? What's going on?"

Principal Koffin stands up at her desk. "Belinda, summon all of Peculiar's witches to the flyball field at once. Let them know it's urgent."

Professor Belinda blinks, like she isn't sure she heard correctly. "*All* the witches in Peculiar? Even the students?"

Principal Koffin nods. "The spell we need will require an immense amount of magic." She walks over to the nearest window and pushes it open. "We're going to need all the help we can get."

The principal climbs out the window, spreads her wings wide, and soars away into the cloudy gray sky.

CHAPTER 10

A storm is brewing above Peculiar, and the chilly, gusty air nips at the noses of Bella, Dee, and all the other witches who gather on the flyball field. There must be at least a hundred of them, Bella observes, some of whom she recognizes from town but didn't even know were witches until now.

"Is that the librarian?" Bella asks Dee, pointing at an elderly woman across the crowd.

"Watch where you point!" Dee pushes her finger down. "You never know what kind of magic might slip out." Then she spots their neighbor and waves. "Hi, Mrs. Cromwell!"

"Don't *worry*," Bella, says zipping her puffy jacket up to her chin. "I have complete control."

Dee frowns just as a crack of thunder booms from the sky like a warning. She looks up, and that's when she notices Crypta and Jeanie walking toward them. Dee tries to turn away like she didn't see, but it's too late.

"Maleficents," Crypta says by way of greeting. "I'm surprised to see you here."

"Every witch in town is here," Bella says. "Where else would we be?"

Crypta shrugs. "Off playing with your dorky friends somewhere. My mother says this is important witch business." She looks to her left, through the crowd, to where

Gretchen Cauldronson appears to be deep in conversation with Principal Koffin and Professor Belinda.

Bella curls her hands into fists by her sides. Dee can sense the angry sparks building up inside her sister and gently touches her arm. "What was it you said about being in control?"

Crypta smirks. By now she's well aware that Bella's magic flares with her temper. "So," Crypta says, changing the subject now that she's gotten under Bella's skin. "Do you know what happened to the veil?"

Bella and Dee look at each other. Gretchen Cauldronson warned them what would happen to their family if they caused one more magical mishap in Peculiar. Crypta was the last person they wanted knowing the truth.

The twins shake their heads.

"No idea," Dee says. "Why would we?"

"Doesn't your mom know?" Bella adds. "Since she knows *everything*?"

Next to Crypta, Jeanie smiles into her chest

like she's trying not to laugh. Crypta shoots her a dirty look.

"No." Crypta says. "All she knows is that the veil is down. But I'll bet she's getting the rest of the story right now. She and Principal Koffin are as chummy as ogres."

Bella's pulse quickens. Would Principal Koffin really tell Gretchen that Bella and Dee were responsible for destroying the veil, knowing it would likely get them expelled from Peculiar?

Thunder roars in the sky again, and this time Dee feels a drop of rain hit her nose.

"Gather round!" commands Principal Koffin, her voice amplified by Professor Belinda's magic. She flaps her wings to hover above the center of the crowd, and everyone stops talking to look up.

"Thank you all for coming. I know you're wondering why I've called you here, so I won't waste any time on pleasantries."

"Does she ever?" Bella whispers to Dee as the rain starts to pick up.

"The veil of protection that has surrounded YIKESSS since its inception has fallen," the principal continues, the wind whipping at her clothes as murmurs run through the crowd. "Restoring it will take a great deal of strength—much more than any one witch is capable of. The only way we will succeed is if we work together. Do I have your support?"

The crowd claps and shouts out their agreement, and Principal Koffin returns to the ground. Professor Belinda, next to her in the center of the crowd, mounts her broom and takes the principal's place in the air.

"Form a circle and join hands," Professor Belinda calls out. "And we shall perform a binding spell to channel our magic into a new protective veil, one even more impenetrable than the last."

Professor Belinda stays still as the crowd of witches disperses to arrange themselves in a circle around her. When the shape is formed, Dee grabs Bella's right hand and Mrs. Cromwell's left, while Bella, much to her chagrin, takes hold of Crypta's hand.

"Join me," Professor Belinda says. She raises an arm straight up in the air and shouts into the sky:

> *"We witches*
> *together as one*
> *call upon the moon and the sun.*
> *Grant us safety and protection,*
> *a veil that cannot be undone."*

She repeats herself, and gradually other witches start to echo the incantation. As the spell grows stronger, white sparks shoot from Professor Belinda's outstretched hand and into the sky, where they reach a peak and burst outward like shooting stars, then fall in an arc that encompasses all of YIKESSS and its surrounding grounds. Slowly, like weaving a sparkling web, the protective veil begins to reknit itself.

"I think it's working!" Bella says, marveling

at the shimmering threads of magic, radiant even through the heavy rain.

"It's beautiful," Dee adds, the sparks shining in her green eyes. "This must be how humans feel when they see fireworks."

"But better," Bella says. From their place at the top of the hill, she can see all the way to the welcome sign at the edge of town, just a tiny pink dot in an expanse of dark green grass. Then something in the sky catches her attention.

"Hey," she says to Dee, gesturing toward the shadowy figure with her chin. "Do you see that?"

Dee squints through the rain to get a better look. "It looks like . . ." She widens her eyes in surprise.

"A harpy," Bella finishes. She can only make out the birdlike woman's silhouette, but there's no mistaking the length of her body, or the expanse of her wings. Her long hair whips around her shoulders as she flutters in place just beyond the veil, watching them.

"I've never seen another harpy in Peculiar before," Dee says. "Or anywhere."

"It looks like Principal Koffin sees her too," Bella says. The twins turn to look at the principal standing in the middle of the circle, her gaze locked on the other harpy. Between the rain and the distance, it's hard to decipher the emotion on her face.

"Hello!" Crypta yanks on Bella's hand. "Sorry to interrupt your little chat, but some of us are trying to save the school!"

"Eat my warts, Crypta," Bella grumbles.

Dee shakes her head at her sister's remark. "No, she's right. We should concentrate." She leans over to Crypta and says, "Sorry." Bella rolls her eyes.

The twins get back to reciting the incantation, focusing on Professor Belinda, who's still leading the group from where she hovers on her broom in the center of the circle. Within a matter of minutes the last threads of magic are woven through the veil and the spell is finished. The witches stop chanting.

"We've done it!" Professor Belinda shouts, and the witches go wild, cheering and hugging and throwing their hats into the air. Amid all the excitement, Bella and Dee search the skies, trying to catch sight of the harpy again, but she's gone. Almost as if she were never there at all.

CHAPTER 11

With the spell complete and the protective veil successfully restored, Professor Belinda leads the soaking wet but cheerful group of witches to the cafeteria for some hot cocoa. On the way, Bella and Dee notice Principal Koffin break away from the group and fly off in the direction of her tower. Feeling remorseful and responsible for this whole mess, the twins decide to forgo the hot chocolate, which they aren't even sure they deserve, to follow her there.

They reach the top of the tower staircase, and the door to the principal's office swings all the way open, as if she were expecting them. They enter silently and sit down on the bench across from the principal's desk.

"Girls," the principal says, though she's standing at the back of the room, facing away from them. Before she can say any more, Dee stands up and clears her throat.

"Principal Koffin, we're so sorry for everything. We meddled where we shouldn't have and ended up putting the whole school in danger."

"I think you mean the entire supernatural community," the principal corrects her, still facing the wall. "The video of the flyball game was a PR nightmare for the Creepy Council. They've been scrambling all day to wipe the memory of every single person who has seen it.

And since it's gone 'viral,' as the humans say, that's been no easy task. Professor Belinda had to beam all the way to Bulgaria!"

Bella puts her head in her hands. "We're going to be expelled from YIKESSS, aren't we?"

Now the principal turns to look at the twins. "How did you get that idea?"

"The Creepy Council warned us that our family would be exiled if we caused any more trouble," Dee reminds her. When the principal doesn't immediately reply, she sits back down. "Aren't you going to tell Gretchen Cauldronson we were the ones who knocked down the veil?"

A look of understanding crosses over the principal's face. "I will not." Her gaze lifts from the twins and floats into the distance. "I'm afraid I don't much see the point in banishing children when they make mistakes. How can we ever expect them to learn if we do not teach them?"

Bella raises her head from her hands. Her face is red and splotchy from crying. "You mean, you protected us?"

The principal cracks the smallest of smiles. "That *is* my job." She looks back at the wall—or rather, at the small portrait of a man and three harpies that hangs there. "You girls told the truth even though it was difficult, because you knew I needed to understand. I suppose I must now do the same for you."

Dee furrows her brow. "What do you mean?"

The principal sits down at her desk. She takes a deep breath. "As you know, the veil of protection is essential for our safety here at YIKESSS. But it doesn't just exist to keep danger out. It also exists to keep me in."

Bella and Dee look at each other, confused.

"What do you—" Dee begins, but the principal holds up a hand to stop her.

"Long ago, in the years before I founded YIKESSS, my life was very different. I did not live in Peculiar, nor did I reside anywhere on the earthly plane at all. In fact, I lived in the Underworld, and I worked for Hades as a Bringer of Vengeance."

Bella tilts her head to the side. "Bringer of . . . what?"

"Who's Hades?" Dee adds.

Principal Koffin looks back at the portrait, but her face doesn't change. "Hades is the king of the Underworld. And I, along with my sisters, Estelle and Magdalene, was responsible for doling out whatever vengeance he brought forth."

"I knew it was you in the portrait!" Bella says. "You look great with your hair down."

"Shh!" Dee swats at Bella.

Principal Koffin remains unamused. "Anytime a monster broke the rules or disobeyed Hades, he would force us to punish them in terrible ways." She looks down at her hands and lowers her voice a little. "I'm not proud to say I carried out these punishments, without question, for many years. Creatures of the Underworld are wild and dangerous, just as Hades likes them to be. Most of the time, I even believed they deserved it." She lifts her head to look directly at the twins. "And then, one day, Hades ordered me to seek vengeance upon a child."

"No way." Bella leans forward in her seat. "A child who lived in the Underworld? What did they do?"

"And what was the punishment?" Dee says.

"Banishment," the principal replies. "And it does not matter what he did. No child ever deserves to be taken away from their loved ones. That's what I told Hades. I refused to send the child away from his family."

"And then what happened?" Dee asks eagerly.

"And then . . ." The principal's voice turns grave. "Hades sentenced me to imprisonment."

Dee covers her mouth with her hand.

"But you were doing the right thing," Bella says. "That's not fair!"

"I managed to escape the Underworld before Hades could get to me. He cannot set foot on earth, you see. Still, I crossed continents and oceans to separate myself from the entrance—a portal in the middle of the Black Sea. I decided to settle in Peculiar when I met a powerful witch who offered to help me by erecting a veil that would make all beneath it invisible and impenetrable. She cast the veil over an abandoned building, which I converted into a sanctuary for wayward monsters, and then, eventually, into a school. That's how YIKESSS was born."

"Wow," Dee marvels. "So you've been hiding here ever since?"

Principal Koffin nods. "That's right."

"But wait," Bella says. "If you can't leave, how did you chaperone the PPS fall dance?"

"The temporary veil that Professor Belinda cast over the public school," the principal explains. "It didn't have the same power or permanence as the YIKESSS veil, but it did the trick for just one night."

"*That's* why you said no to Vice Principal Archaic when he asked you to lunch," Bella says, understanding now. "You can't leave the veil. You have to stay hidden."

The principal nods again. "Hades has spies everywhere, and none better than my sisters. They looked for me for many years after I fled, and are still looking today. The gods are unforgiving that way."

Bella nudges Dee. "That's who we saw flying in the sky when the veil was being repaired!" She points at the portrait, to the sister on the far right.

"Magdalene, yes," Yvette says, a tinge of sadness in her voice. "My younger sister. She's the fastest of the three of us. Hades regularly sends her on scouting missions, but because of the veil, she's never been able to find me."

Dee looks down at her lap. "Until now."

"Because of us," Bella adds, equally glum. "We *really* screwed up."

The principal looks from Bella to Dee. "You did. But that doesn't mean all hope is lost. The veil has been restored and is stronger than ever." She pauses, giving the twins a chance to perk up a little. "Still, we will have to be extra vigilant now that Magdalene knows my location. When she returns to the Underworld, she will report her findings to Hades, and he will surely stop at nothing to take down the veil, and me with it."

Bella shakes her head in disbelief. "I can't believe your sisters would do that to you." She glances at Dee. Her sister is her best friend—her partner in crime. Dee would never betray her. It makes Bella sad that Principal Koffin can't say the same.

The principal looks down at her hands. "We have a complicated relationship. Hades has done many awful things, but he's also a father figure to us. He has provided for us, given us everything the Underworld has to offer. They don't understand why I would give all that up to save a single child."

She stands and walks back to the portrait. "This is the last picture I have of the three of us together. It was a gift from Hades, painted by Michelangelo on a visit to the Underworld.

It was the only thing I had time to grab before I fled." She looks at the twins. "This time of year is usually very hard for me. It's the anniversary of my exile." She moves to the front of her desk and leans against it. "Despite our differences, I still care for my sisters very much. I wish things could be different between us."

"So *that's* why you've been so cranky!" Bella realizes. The principal sends her a look of warning, and she backtracks. "Er—not *cranky*, really. Just a little less chipper than usual." She smiles innocently.

A wistful expression crosses the principal's face. "I am sorry for my misplaced anger. And furthermore, I want to thank the two of you. I know the broken veil put us all in danger, but because of it, I got to see my sister for the first time in more than three hundred years." She smiles at the twins.

"Um," Bella says. "You're welcome?"

"That's okay, Principal Koffin," Dee says. "If

I didn't see Bella for three hundred years, I'd probably be pretty upset too."

"Probably?" Bella says. "You know you'd be miserable without me."

Dee smiles at her sister. "I know."

"Oh!" Bella tries not to get her hopes up too high when she asks, "So now that the veil is back up, does this mean the Harvest Moon Feast is back on?"

The principal nods. "I suppose it does."

"And we aren't going to get into any trouble for telling the truth?" Dee asks. She stands up, hoping they can get out of there before Principal Koffin has any time to think about a punishment.

But the principal gives them a knowing look, stopping them in their tracks. "Not so fast." She looks back at Argus, who until now has been perched quietly with his four eyes closed. He opens his eyes, caws once, and flies to the closet in the back corner of the room. He disappears inside for a few moments, and when he returns, he carries a bucket in his talons, filled to the brim with sponges.

"No!" Dee jumps back in horror. "Expel me if you have to, but *please*, don't make me scrub any more cauldrons!"

Then, for the first time all week, Principal Koffin laughs. "These aren't for you," she says, as Argus flies past the twins and sets the bucket down by her feet. The sponges, glowing with magic, start spilling out and scrubbing the office floor on their own.

"*Phew*," Dee says, the color returning to her face.

"You'll be scrubbing cauldrons this week, though," Principal Koffin says casually, examining her talons. "*And* next. Let the punishment serve as a reminder that interfering in others' lives, when your opinions are neither warranted nor wanted, can lead to dangerous consequences."

Bella sighs. "Fine. I've already blown my

chances at getting on Horror Roll for the quarter, anyway."

"Our hands are going to turn into actual prunes," Dee says. She looks up at Principal Koffin. "But I guess that's our own fault. We took it too far this time."

"We should probably apologize to Vice Principal Archaic, too," Bella says. "I wonder if he's still in his office."

"I believe he is," Principal Koffin replies. "You can stop by on your way to get some hot cocoa."

Bella smiles. "You mean, we get to have some too?"

"With marshmallows and everything?" Dee adds.

"Of course," the principal replies. "You'd best be on your way before it gets cold."

The sisters leave the principal's office arm in arm, excited for hot cocoa and glad the worst is behind them. Principal Koffin watches them go with a melancholy expression on her face.

Argus caws and lands on her shoulder. He nuzzles the top of his head into her cheek.

"I know," she murmurs, stroking the bird's back. "I miss them too."

The principal turns away from the door, and it closes softly behind her.

CHAPTER 12

In the middle of the night, Bella awakens
to find a glowing marble of light hovering
inches from her face.

"What the—" She sits up, shielding her eyes.

"It's me," Dee says softly, kneeling next to
Bella's bed. She cups the tiny ball of light like
precious porcelain in her hands. "I can't sleep."

Bella scoots over in bed and lifts the covers so Dee can get under them. "Did you have the nightmare about the giant spider again?"

Dee gets comfortable in Bella's bed while still carefully handling the light. If she loses focus for even a second, it will go out. "No," she says. "I just can't stop thinking about everything that's happened."

Bella turns onto her side so she's facing Dee. "You mean like how we accidentally knocked down a three-hundred-and-thirty-year-old magical veil with just one potion? Or how, because of us, the king of the Underworld knows where Principal Koffin has been hiding? *Or* how you tamed a room full of plants enchanted with chaos magic?"

Dee nods into the light. "You've been thinking about it too."

"Uh-huh." Bella pulls the comforter up to her chin. "How could I not?"

"Well, how did we do it?" Dee glances at Bella, and the ball of light flickers but doesn't go out. "I mean, we put everyone we know in danger, and we didn't even *mean* to."

"I know." Bella's eyes widen. "Imagine the kind of stuff we could do on purpose."

"That's my point," Dee says, and the light flickers again. "We've got power, Bella. *Real* power that neither of us knows how to control." She pauses a moment to refocus on the light, and its glow seems to strengthen. "It's scary, don't you think?"

Bella shakes her head. "Power doesn't scare me." She rolls onto her back and stares up at the ceiling with a smile growing on her face. "Just *think* about everything we'll be able to do once we master the craft. All the places we can go, and the humans we can influence. All the good we can do for supernaturalkind."

"And humankind," Dee adds, thinking, for a second, of Sebastian.

"Yeah," Bella says. "Them too. It's exciting to think about, isn't it?"

Dee smiles a little as she considers Bella's words. "I guess it's not all bad. We could spell every shelter cat into a loving home."

"Exactly," Bella says. "We can make the world a better place."

Dee's smile falters as she thinks about the veil again. "Or we could destroy the world." The ball of light starts to flicker more aggressively. "What if another one of our spells goes awry, and it's even worse than last time? What if we ruin everything?"

Bella's reply is immediate. "We won't."

"*Meow*," Cornelius cries across the room, from the foot of Dee's bed. The flickering light is disturbing his rest.

"But how can you be so sure?" Dee asks, still not convinced.

Suddenly the light goes out. The sisters lie, still and quiet, in the dark.

"Because we have each other," Bella says finally. "And all the magic in the world can't change that."

Dee finds Bella's hand under the blanket. Bella takes her sister's hand and squeezes back.

WITCHES of PECULIAR

GLIMPSE THE FUTURE

LUNA GRAVES

In Peculiar, Pennsylvania, it is common knowledge among monsters and humans alike that the best place to get a milkshake any day of the week is Scary Good Shakes. The diner, located at 16 Main Street, has been operating since the 1980s, when a witch named Beatrice Wednesday bought the empty building a few blocks down from Ant and Ron's pharmacy and transformed it into the town's premiere destination for frozen desserts.

Nobody knows whether it's a spell that makes Beatrice's milkshakes so tasty or whether she simply has a way with a blender. In all her years running Scary Good Shakes, she has never shared her secret recipe, no matter how big the bribe or pleading the puppy-dog eyes may be. This bothers some people, especially her competitors, but it has never bothered Dee Maleficent. She thinks—she *knows*—that Beatrice makes the best strawberry shakes in the entire universe, and that's good enough for her.

It's a drizzly Saturday morning and Dee is seated in the back of her dads' van, daydreaming about one of Beatrice's strawberry milkshakes with hot fudge on top. She looks out the window, past the raindrops, where she can see a house with a sign posted in the front window that reads LET'S GO PPS PORCUPINES! Behind the house, in the distance, she sees YIKESSS up on the hill.

Principal Koffin's tower ascends into thick fog that, to Dee, looks a lot like whipped cream. A grumbling sound comes from her stomach.

"I'm *starving*," she says. "I might have to order two milkshakes when we get there."

"You're going to turn into a milkshake," Ron replies, smiling at his daughter through the rearview mirror. "How about some scrambled eggs, too?"

"I still can't believe Scary Good Shakes serves breakfast now," Bella says, scrolling on her pink eyephone in the middle seat next to Dee. She shows her screen to Charlie, who's seated on her other side, and they both giggle.

"The perfect end to a totally wicked sleepover!" Eugene remarks from the row of seats all the way in the back. He and Charlie spent the night at Bella and Dee's house, where they cooked homemade pizzas, coordinated and filmed an elaborate skit to post on Bella's WitchStitch account, and had a *Space Wars* movie marathon.

Eugene grips the headrest in front of him and bounces eagerly in his seat. "Man, I have no idea *what* I'm going to order. Do I go savory or sweet? Do I get a side of hash browns, bacon, or toast? Or do I get *french* toast?"

"You sure you're not a werewolf?" Ron jokes from behind the wheel, as Eugene certainly has the appetite of one.

"You can order as much food as you want, Eugene." Antony smiles at him from the passenger seat. He's wearing his human makeup. "I've heard the pancakes are delicious."

"Who knew Beatrice could make delicious pancakes, too?" Dee says, still looking out the window as they turn onto Main Street. She's thinking maybe she'll order some strawberry pancakes to go with her strawberry shake.

"Oh, I forgot to tell you: Beatrice retired," Ant says. "A new family owns Scary Good Shakes now."

Dee's shriek is so earsplitting that Ron slams on the brakes and yells, "WHAT HAPPENED?"

The driver in the car behind them honks their horn.

"Donna!" Ant's left arm is extended out to the side, a reflex to want to protect them all. "What have we said about overreacting when Pop is trying to concentrate?" He regains his composure and says to Ron, "Go, hon. That horn is giving me a headache."

"Overreacting?" Dee's face is a mix of shock and horror. "I'm never going to have another one of Beatrice's strawberry milkshakes *ever* again and you think I'm *overreacting*?"

"Yes," Bella says, not even bothering to glance up from her phone.

"Come on, Dee, you can't be that surprised," Eugene says. "The woman was ancient even when I was a baby."

"So what?" Dee says, and her tone comes out sharper than she intends it to. "That doesn't mean anything. Witches can live for a long time."

"Maybe she gave the new owners her secret recipe," Charlie says optimistically. "She knows how much her milkshakes mean to the town."

Dee says nothing. She crosses her arms and turns away.

The eye on Bella's phone closes, and she puts it down on her lap. "So who are the new owners, anyway?"

"The Nelson-Pans," Ron says. "A husband and wife with two kids. They moved to town a few weeks ago. Dad and I met them last week and told them about the PSBS. They're excited for the next meeting."

Ant and Ron have been members of the PSBS, or Peculiar Small Business Society, for nearly a decade. Any small business owner in town, human or monster, is invited to join.

"Are they witches like Beatrice?" Bella asks.

Ron and Ant exchange a wary glance.

"They're humans," Ant says. He turns to look directly at Bella. "But they're perfectly fine people, so you be nice. I mean it, Bella Boo."